DEADLY DANGER

A SEEING COLORS MYSTERY BOOK 2

J. A. WHITING

D1377768

To hear about new books and book sales, please sign up for my mailing list at: www.jawhiting.com

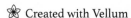 Created with Vellum

For my family with love

1

It was the first day of July and the sun shone down from the bright blue sky over the seaside town of Bluewater Cove on the North Shore of Massachusetts. Holding the leash of her light brown Labrador-poodle mix, Iris, Ellen "Nell" Finley walked beside her sister as they strolled along the brick sidewalks next to the harbor. Sailboats, windsurfers, and paddle-boarders plied the water and people stood near the water's edge taking photographs of the idyllic scene.

"What a beautiful day," Violet said with a wide smile. "We should go to the beach later this afternoon."

"Fine with me. I can try out my new boogie

board," Nell agreed. "Want to ride on the board with me, Iris?"

The dog looked up at Nell and gave a soft, happy woof to indicate her agreement.

"Why don't we walk over to the park?" Violet suggested. "Iris can play with the other dogs while we sit in the shade under the trees."

The sisters left the harbor-side and walked along the sidewalk of the pretty town peeking in the windows of the shops and enjoying the early summer bustle of the tourist season.

When they reached the park, Nell unclipped the leash from the dog's collar and Iris trotted over to the hill to greet the three dogs running and playing there. Nell and Violet sank onto the grass under the tall shade tree. The sisters had been up early to take a twelve-mile bike ride on the paths in the state park before the heat of the day kicked in.

Nell was an artist and graphic designer, and Violet designed and made custom jewelry and pottery. Together they ran a shop in town selling their wares in part of the house they'd inherited from their mother almost a year ago.

The house had been in the family for decades and the Finley family used it every summer and on many weekends, and after their mother died, the sisters decided to turn the section of the house that faced Main Street into their workshop and retail store, and make the rest of the house their permanent home.

"Look, the ice cream truck is here." Nell stood and looked at her sister. "The usual?"

With a smile, Violet nodded and her sister hurried over to get some ice cream for the two of them.

When Nell returned with the cones and a bottle of water, she was surprised to see Iris and a medium-sized, brown dog standing next to Violet. Iris was licking the dog's face which seemed to be a mixed breed with some Labrador and maybe a bit of beagle combined.

"Who's this?" Nell asked handing a cone to her sister. "Hi, dog. Did you make friends with Iris?"

Iris moved close to Nell and nudged at the water bottle in her hand.

"This dog seems to be alone." Violet scanned the park for someone who might be looking for their dog.

Nell noticed the brown dog licking his lips and staring at the bottle so she knelt, opened the container, poured some water into the palm of her hand, and offered it to the canine. He cautiously stepped forward and sniffed Nell's hand, and then greedily drank from her palm.

"Do you think he's lost?" Violet asked.

Nell poured out the water several more times until the dog seemed satisfied, and then she reached her fingers out for the dog to smell. Lifting the dog's tag on his collar, she read it out loud. "Oscar." Nell read off the address and a telephone number. "He lives in Saxonwood." Looking at the dog, she asked, "Is your name Oscar? What are you doing in Bluewater? Where are your people?"

The dog's tail thumped against the grass.

"Read the phone number to me again," Violet said. "I'll call them."

When she made the call, it rang and rang and no one answered. "We can't just leave him here. Should we walk him home?"

Nell looked up the address on her phone. "It will take us about thirty minutes to get there."

"I noticed this same dog in the park the past two days while I was running," Violet said. "Both times it was early in the morning and now he's here in the afternoon. Has he been here for three days?"

Oscar's fur was slightly ratty-looking and Nell wondered how the dog had become separated from his owners. As she was looking down at the dog, his brown fur began to shimmer red, then it turned to a dark burnt orange. The color flickered, and the dog turned black.

An involuntary shiver made Nell's body tremble and Violet hurried to her side and took her arm. "What is it? Is something wrong?"

Nell slammed her eyelids shut and whispered to her sister, "Something ... something isn't right. But I don't know what it is."

THERE ARE some people in the world who have a fourth type of cone in their eyes, and those extra cones allow these people to see many, many more colors than the ordinary person. The people who carry this genetic difference are called tetrachromats.

From the time she was a little girl, Nell used multi-colors to create her artwork. She would draw a beach where the grains of sand would consist of blues, reds, greens, and yellows ... the sky wasn't only a wash of blue, but a mix of gold and silver, with pinks, lavenders, and violet. When Nell's mother asked why she put so many colors into things, Nell told her it was because that was what she saw.

The young girl drew and painted the way she did because she was capable of seeing *millions* more colors than the average person was able to perceive.

A month ago, Nell saw a woman come into their shop, a woman who was colored red from head to toe as if someone had put a filter over her. When the woman left the store, she crossed the street and was hit and killed by a car. Murdered, actually.

Nell's doctor held the theory that she had been able to see emotions such as danger and rage because those things were given off by people as energy and Nell's special visual skills allowed her to see that energy as colors.

Violet put her arm around her sister's shoulders. "Are you seeing something?"

Nell opened her eyes and sucked in a quick breath. She kept her voice low and soft. "There are colors on the dog."

"What colors do you see?" As she spoke, Violet's eyes moved quickly to the lost dog.

When Nell reported what she was seeing, Violet asked, "Red means anger, right? I remember that orange means caution or a warning, but what does black mean?"

Nell hesitated and it took her several seconds to answer. "Some of the things black can stand for are ... evil ... and death."

"Oh, no," Violet muttered. "Oh, no." Leaning down, she petted the dog. "What happened, Oscar? Did something happen at your house? Where are your people?" Turning to her sister, she asked, "Should we go to the house and see if anyone answers?"

A tightness wrapped around Nell's body. "I don't think that's a good idea. Not alone anyway."

"I'll call Peter," Violet said taking her phone from the pocket of her shorts.

Peter Bigelow was a Bluewater Cove police officer who dated the sisters' friend, Dani. Peter knew Nell was a tetrachromat and that for some reason her skill had taken an unusual turn, so last month, he suggested to the police chief that she might be able to assist them with a crime that had occurred in town. Peter's idea proved to be a good one when Nell's perceptive ways pointed her to a killer.

In less than fifteen minutes, Peter arrived at the park in his cruiser and strode across the grassy lawn to where Nell, Violet, Iris, and Oscar were waiting for him. Thirty years old, the young man was tall and slim with broad shoulders that were the result of having been a competitive swimmer for years. He had dark brown hair and friendly blue eyes.

"This is the dog?" Peter asked.

"He's very friendly," Violet said. "I've seen him here in the park the past three days. He's always alone. Nell saw some colors on his fur."

Nell's forehead shimmered with nervous perspiration as she reported which colors she saw shining on the dog's coat. "Maybe something happened to his owners."

"Are the colors still there?" Peter asked eyeing the dog.

"Faintly."

"He doesn't seem injured," Peter observed. "He's been moving fine?"

Nell nodded. "He was very thirsty."

"Maybe we should drop him off at the animal shelter before paying a visit to the address printed on his dog tag."

"Can that wait?" Nell's green eyes looked heavy with worry. "If no one is at the house, I think Violet and I should take him home with us. We can have a vet check him out. If he's been through some traumatic thing, I'd like him to stay with us." She looked to her sister who gave a nod. "He's made friends with

Iris. It might make him less stressed to be with us until his owners can be located."

"It's a good idea," Violet agreed.

"Fine. I'll contact the shelter to see if anyone has reported a missing dog," Peter said. "Why don't we take a ride over to Saxonwood? Maybe someone is at home now and the dog can be reunited with the family."

Violet rode in the front passenger seat while Nell took the rear with a dog on each side of her. The fifteen-minute drive followed the road along the shore before turning inland through a heavily wooded section of Bluewater and into the neighboring town of Saxonwood.

Peter eased the cruiser to a stop in front of a large white Colonial house with black shutters set a little back from the street on a slight hill. The lawn was mowed and there were two flower pots standing at the sides of the front steps. The place looked nicely-tended, but the blooms drooped from lack of water and the warm temperatures.

Oscar wouldn't get out of the car despite both of the sisters' encouraging words to him. When she saw that the brown dog had no intention of leaving the car, Iris jumped back inside.

Nell groaned. "Okay, fine. Stay there, but if

someone comes to the door of that house, you both need to get out."

They left the dogs in the car with the windows rolled down and then Peter led the way to the front door where he pushed on the doorbell. They heard the bell's ring from inside the house.

No one came to see who was calling.

Peter rang the bell again.

Still no one.

"Maybe they're at work," Nell suggested.

Violet called the phone number again, but was met with the empty ringing sound.

"We could leave a note," Peter said and pulled a small pad from his shirt pocket.

"I don't know," Nell said. "Should we call the Saxonwood police? Tell them we'd like a wellness check done?"

"Hold up a minute." Violet looked across the lawn to the next house. "Here comes the neighbor."

2

———

"Hello, there." A short, heavyset man with a bald head who looked to be in his sixties walked decisively across the grass towards Peter, Nell, and Violet. "Has anyone answered the bell?"

"No one seems to be at home." Peter introduced himself.

"I'm Scott McKenzie," the man said. "May I ask why a police officer is knocking on my neighbor's door? Is everything okay? Is Adam okay?"

"We're looking for your neighbor," Peter explained. "His dog has been hanging around in a Bluewater Cove park for the past three days."

"Oscar? In Bluewater?" Scott asked, his face a mix of surprise and worry. "Is Oscar all right?"

Peter said, "He seems to be doing just fine. He's in the cruiser. He didn't want to get out."

Scott glanced to the car parked at the curb. "I haven't seen Adam for three days. How did Oscar happen to be in Bluewater?"

"We don't know. We were hoping someone would be at home," Peter said.

"What's your neighbor's last name?" Nell asked. She'd been scanning the outside of the house and the grounds trying to pick up on anything that might be floating on the air.

"Timson. Adam Timson." Scott's face looked pinched and tight.

"Do you know where Mr. Timson might be?" Peter asked. "Might he be at work?"

"Adam works from home." Scott arched his neck trying to take a peek in through the front window of his neighbor's house.

"What does he do for work?" Nell asked.

"Adam does website design. He has an MBA. He teaches some online business classes for a couple of colleges."

"Do you know which colleges he works for?"

Scott shrugged. "I really don't."

"You said you hadn't seen Adam for a few days,"

Violet said. "Does he leave town a lot? Does he have to travel for his work?"

"Only once in a while. He has clients all over the state."

"Is Adam married?" Nell asked. "Any kids?"

"Adam is single. No kids. He lives alone, well, not quite alone, he has Oscar, of course."

"Do you have any idea why the dog has been in the park for three days?"

"I have no idea." Scott shook his head like he was trying to shake off water. "I don't know where Adam is. He left three days ago in the late afternoon. He had a duffle bag. He let Oscar into the backseat of his car. I was doing some yard work. I waved and walked over. Adam seemed to be in a hurry. He said he'd be back in a day or two. He wanted a few days to himself."

"Did you ask where he was going?" Violet questioned.

"I did ask, but I don't think Adam heard me. At any rate, he didn't reply. He got in the car, said good-bye, and drove away. I called after him to ask if I should take care of his mail, but he just waved at me as he left the driveway."

"What does Adam drive?" Peter asked.

"He drives a silver Honda. A small SUV."

"Do you have his phone number?" Peter asked the neighbor.

"Sure." Scott rattled it off from memory.

"That's the number that's on Oscar's dog tag," Nell pointed out. "My sister called a couple of times, but no one answered."

"No? I wonder why he doesn't pick up?" Scott pondered.

"Does Adam have any relatives?" Peter asked.

"Um. Yeah. He mentioned a sister. I don't recall her name." Scott rubbed the back of his head. "I don't know if there's anyone else. I don't know if Adam ever told me what town his sister lives in. Maybe he didn't."

"Have you met the sister?" Violet asked. "Has she come down to visit?"

"No, I haven't met her. I'm not sure if she's been down here or not, but I've never seen her." Scott drew in a long breath. "I'm sorry, I'm not much help."

"You're quite a lot of help." Peter was writing some notes on a small pad. "Can you tell us how long Adam has lived here?"

"About a year and half. My wife and I have been here for over ten years. It's a nice street, quiet, lots of trees, privacy."

Peter looked up from his notetaking. "Do you happen to have a key to the house?"

"I don't. When Adam was going to be away from home all day, he asked me to let Oscar out. I have the code to the garage door. I use that to get into the garage. Adam leaves the door from the garage to the kitchen unlocked so I just open it and call to the dog to come out. There was no need for a key."

"I'm going to walk around the perimeter of the building right after I call the Saxonwood police department," Peter informed everyone. "I'd like an officer to come down and have a look around inside the house and garage."

Scott's wife, Sheryl, sixty-years-old, blond, short and slim, came hurrying towards the group. "What's going on? Why is an officer at Adam's house? Has something happened to Adam?"

"No, nothing's wrong," Scott explained to his wife. "Oscar has been alone in Bluewater for three days. He was in a park. The officer found him and brought him home. They'd like to locate Adam, but he's not answering his phone."

"Where on earth did Adam go off to?" Sheryl stood with a hand on her hip, her blue eyes flashing. "And why isn't Oscar with Adam? How did the dog get lost in Bluewater?"

"Could Adam be in Bluewater?" Nell asked Sheryl hoping the wife might know more than her husband.

"I don't know where he is," Sheryl said. "He could be anywhere as far as I know."

"Are you friendly with Adam?" Violet asked the woman.

"I can't say Scott and I are friends with Adam. We're friendly, neighborly. We let the dog out for him when he's going to be late getting home. We take his mail in if he goes away for any length of time. We chat when we're in the yard."

"Does he have visitors? Do friends come over?" Nell questioned. "Is there a girlfriend?"

"Sometimes there's a car in his driveway, probably a friend over for a visit. Only once in a while though, not very often. My guess is Adam goes out to socialize with friends. He seems to like his privacy."

Nell cocked her head slightly to the side. "Why do you say that?"

"Adam is a quiet man," Sheryl said. "He never has a woman over, barely has anyone visiting him. He does his work, takes care of the house, takes Oscar for walks. He seems to live a simple life. No flashy cars or clothes. In the summer, I see him reading on his back porch. I just get the impression Adam prefers the quiet life."

"Did Adam like his dog?" Nell asked.

"He dotes on that dog. He loves Oscar," Sheryl told her.

Peter got off the phone with the town's police department. "An officer from Saxonwood will be here shortly to do a check on the house."

"Why?" The news seemed to alarm Sheryl.

"Because Adam's dog was lost in the next town from here for three days. No one knows where Adam is and he isn't answering his phone. We just want to be sure Adam didn't return home and fall ill." Peter spelled out their concerns. "So the officers will check things out. The police will also call the hospital and check around town to be sure there wasn't an accident."

Sheryl's hand covered her mouth. "An accident? Oh, gosh. Let's hope Adam is enjoying himself some-where and hasn't run into some kind of trouble."

"I'll walk the periphery. I'd like all of you to stay in the front yard." Peter took a few steps away before looking back. "Nell, would you mind accompanying me?"

Nell hesitated for a moment and then stepped forward. "Sure. Sure, I'll go along with you."

Once they were away from Scott and Sheryl, Peter asked, "Did you see any colors on the house or on the couple?"

"Only a tiny bit of pale red on the husband and wife," Nell said. "That color seems to come from nervousness and worry. I also saw tiny little flashes of black."

"What's black stand for?" Standing on his tiptoes, Peter looked into the house through the window.

"It can stand for a few things. Mystery is one of them. In this case, it might represent the mystery of where and why Adam has left his home for a few days. It can also represent evil ... and death."

Peter gave Nell a quick look. "Great. I'm glad the other officer is on his way. We're in their jurisdiction so they can talk it over and figure out what's going on around here."

"Do you think something is going on?" Nell asked the question.

"I have no idea." Peter moved to look in through the next window. "I suppose Adam might have stopped in Bluewater for a bite to eat or a bottle of water, or to get some gas. The car door opened and the dog took off."

"Why would he take off?" Nell asked.

Pressed close to look into another window, Peter shaded his eyes from the glare. "I don't know. The dog spotted a cat. He wanted to run around. He needed to pee. He was tired of Adam. Who the heck knows?"

"I don't think so," Nell said keeping her eyes averted from the windows not wanting to see anything bad that might be behind the glass.

"Why don't you think Oscar would try to run away?" Peter asked. "If the dog saw a squirrel, he'd probably take off after it. He might have gotten lost. Maybe Adam is feeling bad about his missing dog. Maybe he feels responsible for the dog going missing. Maybe Adam searched all over Bluewater, but just couldn't find him."

"I don't think that's what happened," Nell said.

Peter asked, "Why don't you think so?"

"If you lost your dog in an unfamiliar town, what would you do?"

"I'd look all over for him," Peter told her.

"And if you couldn't find him, what would you do? Just drive away?"

"Of course, not. I'd call the police and report him missing. Maybe I'd put up *lost dog* notices. I'd call the animal rescue to see if someone brought my dog in."

"Exactly," Nell said. "Adam doesn't seem to have done any of those things."

Peter stood still in front of Nell. "Do you think Adam deliberately dumped his dog and took off?"

"That would be a terrible, terrible thing to do." Nell shook her head. "Is that why Oscar didn't want to get out of the car?" The young woman made eye contact with Peter. "Here's another question. Sheryl told me Adam loved Oscar. If Adam abandoned a dog he loved, why did he?"

3

While waiting for the Saxonwood police officer to arrive, Peter went to the cruiser to check-in with the Bluewater police station and to let the dogs out so they could walk around. Nell asked Sheryl to describe Adam Timson for them.

"Well, let's see," the woman said. "Adam is in his early forties, about six feet tall. He has a medium build, not thin, not overweight. He has blond hair and blue eyes. Adam is on the quiet side. He's at home a lot." Sheryl looked at Nell. "What else can I tell you?"

"Do you feel you know him well?" Nell asked.

"No, not well at all." Sheryl asked her husband's

opinion. "What do you think? Would you say you know Adam well?"

"I wouldn't say so. We don't socialize. We just chat about general things mostly. I know a few things about him, but not a whole lot." Scott turned to the street as the police car from Saxonwood pulled up the driveway.

Before the police got out to speak with Peter, Nell asked another quick question. "Do clients come to Adam's house sometimes?"

"I didn't notice, but I would say probably not. I think Adam would prefer to meet clients in town, not in his home."

"Did Adam have an office in town?" Violet asked.

"He didn't. He told me once he met his clients at the library or at the coffee shop or at their offices," Sheryl informed them.

Peter brought over the Saxonwood officer, Mitch Lane, and made introductions.

Iris and Oscar sat in the grass near the driveway and watched the humans. Oscar acted a little nervous and showed no interest in going into his home.

"I hear you're concerned about Mr. Timson." Officer Lane was about thirty, tall, and quite slender. "Does anyone have a key to the house?"

Scott explained that he had the garage door code, but if the kitchen door wasn't unlocked, they wouldn't be able to enter the house.

"Okay," Officer Lane said. "Let's get the garage door opened and we'll see about the kitchen door."

Scott led them to the garage where he punched in the code to raise the door.

Officer Lane tried the door leading inside and to everyone's surprise, it opened.

"Well, that was easy." Officer Lane suggested that Nell, Violet, Scott, and Sheryl wait outside while he and Peter went in to make the inspection of the house.

Nell, disappointed that she wouldn't be allowed in, walked over to sit with the dogs. Oscar moved close to her and leaned against Nell's arm. "It's okay, boy."

She wished she could get inside. The dog's fur looked to her to be tinted a light orange color and she was concerned something happened in the house that had frightened Oscar, causing his reluctance to approach the home he'd lived in with Adam.

Scott and Sheryl, with her arms wrapped around her body, stood off to the side of the house talking with each other, one of them occasionally taking a quick glance to the garage.

"Isn't it odd that Oscar doesn't act like he lives here? If it was Iris, she'd gallop up to the door of the house, eager to be let in."

"I was thinking the same thing. He behaves as if he never lived here at all." Violet eyed the open garage door. "What happened to make Oscar uneasy? Something must have upset him. Thinking about it makes *me* uneasy. I hope Peter and that other officer don't find anything inside." Violet lowered her voice. "Are you seeing colors?"

"Only on Oscar's fur. It's shimmering a soft orange color, sometimes flecks of black and purple show up."

"A warning," Violet said. "But also the color of fear or death. I don't like it. I think we should get out of here and go home."

Just then, the officers came out of the house, and Nell and Violet stood.

"No one's inside," Peter announced right away. "There's nothing unusual in the house. Everything looks normal."

Officer Lane said, "The kitchen has some dirty dishes in the sink. The bed was made, but not done in a fussy way. Nothing looks amiss, just like a home where someone had something to eat and then went out."

"But the dog...." Nell said.

"What's that?" Officer Lane asked. "Oh, right. Maybe the dog decided to take an excursion and ended up in Bluewater. It's not that far away."

Nell exhaled loudly. "But if Adam went away for a few days, why didn't he ask the neighbors to care for Oscar?"

Scott said, "I saw the dog in the car when Adam drove away. He was in the backseat."

"So Oscar was with Adam when Adam left the house," Sheryl said. "How did Oscar wind up in Bluewater? And where is Adam?"

Officer Lane gave a shrug. "Adam probably left the dog with a friend in Bluewater and then the dog got loose and went for a walk."

"Why wouldn't the person report the dog missing?" Nell asked. "Why not call the police or the animal shelter?"

"Not everyone is a responsible person." The officer shook his head. "The dog sitter probably figures the dog will come back when he's ready."

"I'd be pretty angry with that dog sitter," Violet's face had taken on an angry expression.

"People go away all the time. They need some

time alone or want to spend time with a friend or girlfriend. They need a little break."

Sheryl interrupted. "Adam doesn't have a girlfriend."

"A friend then," Officer Lane suggested. "He'll be back when he's good and ready. This happens all the time. He's a grown man. There's no need to worry."

Nell didn't agree. There seemed to be plenty to worry about.

Sheryl and Scott thanked the officer for his time and told Peter, Nell, and Violet how they appreciated them coming by to be sure nothing bad had happened. "If you need anything, we're right next door." The couple returned to their house, and Officer Lane spoke with Peter for a few minutes before heading to his car.

Peter walked to the garage to lower the door. "So, it seems everything is okay," he said.

"Is it?" Nell's eyes ran over the outside of the house.

"Nothing was out of place in there?" Violet asked. "There wasn't any sign of a struggle? Of an attack?"

"Nothing like that," Peter told them.

"What about a notepad on the counter?" Violet

questioned. "Were there any notes anywhere? Sticky notes? A pad of paper?"

"We weren't doing a criminal investigation. It was a wellness check. We were making sure Mr. Timson wasn't inside hurt or ill. We checked to be sure there wasn't any sign of foul play. The house looked normal ... like someone lived there."

"Can we go in?" Nell asked.

Peter stared at her. "Why?"

"I'd like to just get a feel for the house."

"You want to know if you'll see colors in there?" Peter asked.

Nell gave a nod.

Peter looked back to the house, glanced at the neighbor's place, and down at the road. "Okay. Let's make it quick."

"Do you remember the garage door code?" Violet questioned as they hurriedly followed Peter.

"I made sure I watched what it was." He punched in the code and the door went up. "Let's go."

Nell looked back at Iris and Oscar sitting in the driveway watching them. "Come on, dogs. Come with us."

Neither dog moved.

"Stay there then," she said. "Don't leave the yard."

They entered into a remodeled high-end kitchen with big windows over the sink. The floor was glossy and the walls were painted a soft neutral color, but when Nell laid her eyes on them, the walls were covered in red. When she reported her visual experience to her companions, Peter looked uncomfortable.

"What does it mean?" he asked.

"I really don't know. The energy in the room is displaying to me as red. There's a lot of it."

"What does red signify again?" Peter questioned.

Violet walked slowly around the space. "It can mean a lot of different things, but in this case, I'm going to guess what Nell is seeing means anger ... rage."

"It can also mean death," Nell said softly.

"Let's hope the symbolism in here isn't pointing to that," Violet almost shuddered.

Peter led them through the living and dining rooms, into a small den, and then up the stairs to four bedrooms and two baths.

"This is a big house for one guy." Violet opened the closet door to see the clothes lined up neatly along the rack. "This Adam person is too neat."

The master suite and one guestroom were elegantly decorated as if Adam Timson had hired an interior decorator to design the rooms. The other two bedrooms were empty.

"Maybe he ran out of money," Violet suggested.

"Or didn't want to waste his money on furniture that would never be used." Nell walked around the room waiting to see if she'd notice any unusual color shades coming from the walls.

They went down to the basement which was completely empty.

"This sure doesn't look like our basement." Violet stared in amazement at the open space. "Is this what a basement is supposed to look like?" she kidded. "We have stuff overflowing in ours."

"It's definitely not the norm," Nell said. "At least, not by our standards."

"Yeah," Peter agreed. "My cellar does *not* look like this one."

They went into the garage and when Nell spotted the pull-up staircase that led to the overhead storage section, she asked Peter if he would take a look up there.

Peter pulled down the foldable wooden staircase and climbed up. "It's neat up here, too. There's some camping equipment, a pair of snowshoes, and a pair of cross-country skis. That's it." He moved backwards down the stairs.

"Can I go look?" Nell asked.

"Sure, go ahead. Be quick though."

Nell climbed up and looked around at the garage storage space. Tiny orange flashes sparkled like the beam from a lighthouse, shining on and off at regular intervals. "I see some little orange flashes in here."

"A warning?" Peter asked Violet.

"That's what it seems to mean most of the time," she told him.

When Nell climbed down the ladder, Peter asked her if she was finished. "I don't want to linger in here in case Officer Lane comes by again."

Violet thought of an excuse for being inside the house. "We'll just tell him you left a light on upstairs and we came in to turn it off."

Peter turned for the backdoor. "See? Everything is normal in here. And Nell only saw red walls in the kitchen. Maybe Adam had an argument with someone while he was in this room and that's what you're picking up on."

"I'm picking up on something else, too." Nell looked from Violet to Peter.

"What's that?" Peter's forehead was scrunched and lined.

"There aren't any dog dishes in here. No dog bed. Not a single dog toy."

Peter's mouth opened slightly.

Violet turned in a circle trying to locate a dog dish. "Weird. Did Oscar really live here?"

"How can you have a dog, and have no dog dish?" Nell asked, a flutter of nervousness moving over her skin.

4

Nell, Violet, and Peter searched the rooms for any sign that a dog had been living in the place ... looking for bowls or dishes, bags of dog food, a leash, dog brush, a blanket or dog bed, or some toys. Oscar had come inside and was sniffing around the kitchen like he was trying to find his water bowl.

There was nothing.

"Maybe Adam was going away for a lot longer than he told the neighbor he'd be gone," Nell had said.

"Is it possible that Oscar never lived here at all?" Violet wondered out loud.

Peter narrowed his eyes. "If that's the case, then what? The next door neighbors lied about taking care of Oscar when Adam Timson was late getting home or went away somewhere?"

Nell and Violet stood dumbfounded.

"What's going on here?" Violet asked nervously.

Nell said, "Oscar didn't seem to react much when he saw the neighbors. He wagged his tail, but he didn't act like he knew them very well."

"My neighbors have two dogs," Peter said. "They never behave like they know me. They always bark at me until I call their names a few times. I don't think it means much that Oscar didn't act all friendly towards the neighbors."

"Should we talk to the neighbors again?" Violet asked. "Ask if they know where the dog's stuff is?"

"That's probably a good idea. I'll go get them." Peter started for Scott and Sheryl's house.

Nell and Violet kept looking around the house for dog items, and Peter was back with Scott in less than five minutes.

"The dog bowls are always right there next to the refrigerator. Maybe Adam put them away in the closet." The man opened the hall closet door expecting to find the bag of dog food on the floor. He stared into the empty space scratching his head. "There's nothing in here. Adam might have taken the things with him."

"What about a dog bed or blanket?" Nell asked.

"There are two dog beds. One in the master bedroom and one in the den," Scott told her.

When they went to look for them, the spaces were empty.

"Well, I'll be....." Scott let his voice trail off. "Adam must have taken everything when he left." The neighbor blinked at the others. "I suppose he wanted the dog to be comfortable."

"We'll just make do when we get Oscar home with us," Violet said. "We have a lot extra blankets. Oscar can use one of them."

When Scott returned to his house, Violet, Nell, and Peter stood in the driveway talking. Scott was back right away carrying two plates of cooked, cut-up chicken breast.

"Sheryl was going to use this for dinner tonight, but when she heard there wasn't any dog food in the house, she worried Oscar hadn't eaten for a while and sent this over for him and the other dog. Just leave the plates on the back steps. I'll pick them up tomorrow," Scott said before returning home.

Peter had already contacted Officer Lane to explain they'd gone back into Adam Timson's house to look for dog food and a dog bed, but everything was missing. Officer Lane didn't sound very concerned, but told Peter he'd make a note in the report about it.

"Oscar seemed familiar with the house," Nell pointed out. "He seemed confused that none of his things were there."

"Officer Lane thinks Peter just went off for a few days," Violet said, her face turned towards the front door of Adam's home. "I don't think that's the case."

"It's possible. Maybe the guy is just odd in his ways," Peter suggested. "Maybe he always takes the dog's things when he goes away so Oscar will be comfortable."

"Let's say that's what he always does." Nell pushed her long, auburn hair away from her face. "If the man is so obsessed with keeping his dog happy, why didn't he inform the police or the animal rescue when Oscar went missing?"

"The whole thing is a mess." Peter bent to pat Oscar and Iris. "I don't like it. You two have some time? How about we drive around for a while? We have the description of Adam's vehicle."

"You want to see if it's in the area?" Nell asked.

"I got the license plate number when I went to the cruiser earlier. I called the station. They looked it up."

"Okay, then. Let's go."

THE GROUP CRUISED the streets of Saxonwood and then drove around Bluewater.

"Too bad Adam didn't tell Scott where he was headed," Violet said from the front passenger seat. "Then we'd know which direction to drive."

"If Adam was going north or south, he'd probably head to the highway." Peter had already driven the roads that led to the interstate. "Most likely, he's long gone by now."

Nell looked out of the car's back passenger window. She had one arm around Iris and the other around Oscar. "If he was being stealthy, he might take the back roads."

"Why would he be stealthy?" Peter questioned.

"What if Adam was afraid someone wanted to hurt him? He could have been in a hurry to get where he was going," Nell offered. "Maybe the trip was so urgent, he couldn't stay long to search for Oscar. Maybe he had to leave right away, but for some reason, he didn't want to take the highway."

"Why would someone want to hurt him?" Violet questioned.

"I don't have an answer for that," Nell said.

Peter drove in circles around the town until everyone decided to give up.

"I need to use a bathroom." Peter pulled the cruiser into a fast food parking lot and stopped next to a dumpster. "Anyone want anything?"

The sisters declined, and Peter left the car to go into the restaurant.

"The dogs might need to get out and stretch their legs." Nell and Violet opened the doors and Oscar and Iris trotted around the corner of the lot with their heads down sniffing at everything and then they made their way to a weedy patch of grass.

The young women followed the dogs to the rear of the lot.

"Maybe I should go in and use the restroom, too." Violet took a few steps towards the fast food place.

"Wait a second." Nell stood staring. "That car over there. It's the same make and model of the car Adam Timson was driving."

Violet's eyes widened as she saw the vehicle her sister was pointing at. "Is that Adam's car? Is he inside the restaurant? Adam's license plate number is in the cruiser." Violet jogged over to Peter's cruiser and leaned in for the small notepad with the number written on it.

Hurrying back to the silver car, Violet checked the numbers. "Oh, gosh. It *is* Adam Timson's car."

Nell texted Peter telling him to look around inside for a man who matched Timson's description.

When Violet moved towards the vehicle to look through the windows, Nell told her not to get too close. "Wait for Peter. Just in case."

"Just in case of what?" Violet's face looked horrified. "You mean, in case he's in there slumped over or something?"

Nell shrugged, and with a nervous tinge to her voice, she said, "Let Peter handle it."

Peter was out of the restaurant in minutes. "No one inside matches the description of Timson. Stay right here. I'll go back and have another look."

He looked into the vehicle and walked all around it, and then checked underneath the body of the car. "All clear."

"So where is he?" Nell glanced around. "Should we get out of here?"

"Why should we leave?" Violet asked. "If Adam went into one of the other stores, he'll be thrilled to see Oscar when he comes out."

"Because." Nell swallowed hard. "There are colors all over that car."

Violet sidled up next to her sister. "What colors do you see?"

Nell took a step back. "Red, bright red. Orange. Black. Purple. It feels ... *bad* to me. I think we should go."

Peter strode over to the dumpster and climbed up on the metal slats.

"Oh, no," Nell whispered and turned around not wanting to watch.

"You're scaring me, you know," Violet told her.

Peter jumped down.

"He's not in there, is he?" Nell almost shook from anxiety.

Peter walked back to them with the dogs at his heels. "There's no one in the dumpster."

Nell turned to face him.

"But there is something interesting in there." Peter took a quick glance back to the dumpster. "There's a dog bowl. It has the name *Oscar* engraved on it."

Nell's face showed confusion.

"Oscar's bowl is in there?" Violet's face clouded.

"There's also what looks like a dog bed, and there's a bag of dog food in there, too," Peter said.

"What the heck is going on?" Violet demanded even though she knew full well no one could answer her question. "Where's Adam Timson?"

"I need to go sit in the cruiser," Nell said softly.

"Come on," Peter said. "I'm going to call this in. I want to talk to the chief. Timson might show up to get his car and then I can have a conversation with him. He'll probably be overjoyed to see Oscar. But if he doesn't show up soon, we might need to investigate since things are becoming more questionable. We might need to look over the car."

When the people and the dogs were back in the cruiser, Violet leaned her head against the head rest. "Whatever you do, please don't end up telling us Adam's body is in that trunk."

Nell groaned from the backseat.

Peter spoke into the radio reporting his concerns to the police station dispatcher.

"Why would Adam toss Oscar's things into the dumpster?" Violet asked. "Why did he park his car back here behind the fast food place? It's like he's trying to hide it."

Nell took a look out of the window at the stores on the other side of the lot. She had a strong sense that Adam wasn't in any of them. He couldn't have left the negative energy from his emotions all over his car and just be out for a shopping trip.

When she looked in the other direction and across the street, Nell noticed the sign.

"I think I might know why Adam left his car back here," she said.

"Why?" Peter looked at her from the rearview mirror.

Nell sighed. "The bus station's over there. Maybe Adam left town, and if he did, I guess he didn't plan on taking his car with him."

5

I t was late when Nell and Violet returned home with the two dogs. After Oscar had some food and water, Iris acted like a big sister showing him around the house, the deck, and the yard. After the tour, the two of them curled up on the rug and fell sound asleep while the young women talked for hours about the strange afternoon they'd had.

Peter had informed both the Saxonwood and Bluewater police departments about what seemed to be Adam Timson's abandoned car. Officers arrived from the two towns to inspect the vehicle, looking in the windows and checking the closed trunk.

"There's no smell coming from back here," an officer said.

That meant they couldn't detect an odor from a dead body stored in the trunk.

"And there's no sign of blood on the bumper or around the edge of trunk," he told them. "There's no overt sign of foul play that would necessitate us trying to pop the trunk. Maybe Timson parked the car here and went off with a friend intending to come back later to pick it up. There's nothing wrong with that. There's nothing wrong with a guy going off for a while. I think you're making too much of it."

The statement made Nell angry, but she didn't see how arguing with the Saxonwood officer would change his mind, plus she was exhausted from being at Adam's house, driving around looking for the man, and standing in the lot while the police performed their inspection. Everything pulsed with thousands of colors and she longed to go home and sit surrounded by the calming, quiet hues of their rooms.

"They're not putting the details together," Violet had protested, sitting in the living room with her feet tucked up under her and sipping from her cup of tea. "Adam loved his dog, but Oscar was found alone in the park. Three days ago, Adam and the dog were seen driving away from their house. Adam didn't report Oscar missing. We find his car parked behind a fast food place with Oscar's things tossed in the bottom of the nearby dumpster. Tell me how all of that isn't weird ... and cause for concern."

"The police see weird things every day." Nell was resting on her back on the sofa with her eyes closed. "Like they said, there's no law against running off for a while, or for forever. There *is* a law against deliberately abandoning your dog, but that doesn't seem to be what happened." Nell sat up. "Or is it? Did Adam dump his dog on purpose? He threw Oscar's things into the dumpster like he knew he would never see the dog again."

"The neighbor told us Adam loved Oscar." Violet looked across the room at the two dogs sleeping soundly. "Was Adam so despondent over something that he was leaving everything behind? Did he drop Oscar in a public park thinking someone would find him and take care of him? Do you think Adam might be planning to harm himself?"

Nell's green eyes narrowed. "If you were going to abandon your dog, wouldn't you take his collar off? Or at least his dog tag? It pointed right to his house."

"Maybe Adam wanted people to know that he did this on purpose ... so someone would find his body." Violet's face was sad.

Nell's shoulders slumped. "He couldn't be in the

trunk of his own car, could he?"

"Oh, gosh," Violet moaned. "Well, the police said they'd check on the car over the next couple of days. Eventually, they'll figure out if Adam shut himself in his trunk in order to harm himself."

Nell shook her head. "On the other hand, it's more likely Adam was fed up with his life in Saxonwood and decided to take off. Maybe for a few days or maybe permanently."

"Then why wouldn't he drive his car wherever he was going?" Violet asked.

"Good question." Nell leaned back against the sofa.

"Did he own his house or was he renting?" Violet questioned. "If he owns the house, wouldn't he sell it before he took off?"

"Another good question." Nell picked up her tea mug and took a sip. "If he was in a big hurry, he might just contact a real estate agent and tell him or her to put it up for sale. He doesn't have to be here in order to sell it."

"He might have done that already," Violet suggested. "The house could go up for sale any day. But what's the big rush? And wouldn't you spend a little time trying to place your dog somewhere before running off like a damsel in distress?"

Nell turned her head slowly to look at her sister. "Could Adam be in some kind of trouble?"

Violet's eyes widened. "What sort of trouble?"

"It does seem very odd for him to leave Oscar in the park, drive to a fast food place and leave his car, and then go ... somewhere. It's all so rushed, so disorganized." Nell held Violet's eyes. "So desperate."

"What in the world could he have done that made him blast out of town like a torpedo?" Violet asked.

Nell hated to say it. "Something bad? I saw those colors in his kitchen, on the car, and on Oscar. They aren't colors that represent serenity and calm. They indicate anger, chaos, danger, a warning ... death." She ran her hand through her hair. "I don't care what the police think. Something's wrong."

BLUEWATER POLICE CHIEF Alan Lambert was in his mid-sixties, trim and fit, bald, and blue-eyed. Peter had told him about Nell's visual skills as a tetrachromat as well as her sudden and unexpected ability to pick up on energy given off by someone's emotions. Almost two months ago, the chief requested Nell's help on a case and she did her best to provide some insight into the murder. After hearing about the lost dog and the man who seemed to be in such a hurry to leave town, Chief Lambert invited her in for a talk.

Sitting across from the chief in his office, Nell asked, "You heard we had an interesting day yesterday?"

"Indeed, I did. What do you make of it?" The chief leaned forward a little.

Nell explained the colors she'd seen on the dog, in Adam Timson's kitchen, and on Adam's car and she gave her interpretation of their meanings. "I think Adam is worried about something. So worried that he rushed away without making any plans. It seems kind of desperate to me."

She went on to tell the chief everything she remembered from the time she and Violet found Oscar in the park to when they finally left the fast food parking lot. "Adam left his car there. He threw Oscar's things into the dumpster."

Chief Lambert stroked his chin. "If you didn't pick up on the colors, I might be inclined to say the guy decided to make a change and left town. We don't know the man. Maybe he's the type who can leave a dog alone in another town with the belief someone will take him in. Or there's such a need to get away that he doesn't care what happens to the dog. However, the colors you saw give the story a different blush, as does the fact Adam left his car behind. There could be a reason, of course. Perhaps he left with a woman. Maybe she's married and Adam doesn't want anyone to see him in his car. Maybe he took off with someone else and he needs to be anonymous for some reason. There could be reasons why he did what he did and those reasons may not have anything to do with something illegal or criminal."

Nell nodded.

The chief continued. "Still, Adam's behaviors cause some concern. Is he in a delicate mental state that could result in him harming himself? *Did* he do something illegal or criminal? I'm having an officer check the car every day. We're going to do a few more things. If things turn out to be suspicious, we'll push a little more."

"What are you planning to do?" Nell watched the man's face.

The chief tapped a pencil on top of a pad of paper. "I want to know if Adam owns that house. I'd like to talk to his friends and anyone he might have been dating. I'd like to speak with some of his clients or business associates. Did Adam have debts? Was he a gambler? Was he into anything illegal? Was he involved with drugs? That's for starters. Depending on the answers we discover, we'll either move forward with an investigation to try and find the man or we'll just let it lie and assume Adam decided to make a change."

When the chief said *we*, a shiver of nervousness rode over Nell's skin. Does he mean *we* as in me?

"Can you spare some time? Would you be able to accompany Peter on some interviews?" the chief asked. "Please don't feel pressured to say *yes*."

"Um." Nell wasn't sure if she could be of any use. "I'd be glad to go along if you think it would be helpful."

"I do think it would be helpful. If you can fit into your schedule, I'd appreciate it."

Tipping her head to the side, Nell made eye contact with the chief. "What does this situation feel like to you? What do you think is going on?"

Chief Lambert let out a breath of air before speaking. "Sure, people run off. People do things on the spur of the moment. Some people do things without thinking, others plan things meticulously. But this doesn't feel right to me. I think something is wrong. Very wrong."

6

Peter drove the cruiser and Nell sat in the passenger seat as they made their way to the town of Saxonwood.

"Adam Timson owns the house he lives in. He's owned it for about a year and a half." Peter checked the rearview mirror before changing lanes. "He had a small loan on his car. Other than that and the mortgage, he has no debt."

"So he probably isn't a gambler, right?"

"It seems not. It doesn't seem like he was dating anyone either. The man lives a very boring life."

Nell shook her head. "Adam's boring life might have changed recently. I don't think it was boredom that chased him out of town."

"Maybe not. What was it then?" Peter asked.

Nell looked up at the sky. Heavy dark clouds were moving in obscuring the blue of the morning. "Are we supposed to get a storm?"

Almost a year ago, Nell was in central Massachusetts cleaning out their mother's house after she had passed away when a sudden and unexpected storm came up. Not just a storm ... a tornado ... an F-4 tornado that blew the entire house away leaving Nell crouched in the basement quaking in fear, drenched from the wild, pelting rain, terrified for her life. Twenty-four people died that afternoon from the kind of storm that is never seen in Massachusetts. Until that day.

Now Nell panicked any time bad weather threatened, and when a storm did hit, she had to sit in the basement in a rocking chair with Iris's sweet head on her lap repeating to herself that she'd be okay, everything would be okay, until it was over.

Peter pulled the cruiser into a lot and parked. "Adam did a lot of work for this guy we're seeing ... he created a website, did graphic design. Let's see what we can learn from him."

Ed Barnes stood when he saw them come into the café and he shook hands with Peter and Nell. The man was tall, over six feet, sturdy and strong-looking. He had short brown hair and was about forty years old.

"Thanks for meeting with us," Peter said. "You've spoken already with an officer from Bluewater?"

"That's right. Over the phone. Is there any word about Adam?"

"Not yet. I'm sure we'll know something soon," Peter said. "I'd like to ask some questions, if you don't mind. Some will be the same as the ones the officer asked you over the phone."

Ed nodded. "Anything I can help with."

"Did Adam ever say anything about going away for a while?"

"Not to me, no. He didn't tell me anything about a trip or plans to get away." Ed's expression was one of alarm. "Can you tell me why the police are involved? Do you think something happened to Adam?"

"His dog was found in Bluewater and his car was located behind a fast food restaurant. It seems he left his house in haste. We're hoping to locate Mr. Timson in case he needs some help."

"What sort of help? Is he in danger?" Ed asked.

"We have no reason to believe that," Peter reassured the man. "We'd just like to locate Mr. Timson in case he's feeling despondent over something."

Nell watched Ed carefully. He was giving off short waves of a yellow-red color. She didn't need to see the colors around him to know Ed was worried and anxious about Adam's absence.

"Did Adam seem himself when you were with him last?" Peter asked.

"Yes, he did. We met at my office to go over a new website design he was doing for me." Ed looked down at his mug replaying the meeting in his mind. "Adam seemed normal. Nothing seemed different about him. He's a quiet man in general, friendly, polite, not loud or extroverted. He's easy to get along with. The last time I saw him, he was the same as always."

"Did he seem distracted at all? Forgetful?"

Ed shook his head. "Not at all."

"Did he ever mention concerns about money?"

"Not to me."

"What about trouble with anyone? A difficult client? A run-in with anyone?"

"I don't know anything about that. I never heard any concerns like that from Adam."

"Was Adam dating anyone?" Nell asked.

"He never mentioned dating. He never talked about a wife or a girlfriend."

"How long had Adam done work for you?" Peter asked.

"Let's see. It's been almost a year."

"Did you talk about things not related to work?"

"Sure. We'd talk about sports, stuff going on in town, I'd tell him what my kids were up to, where we were going on vacation, things like that," Ed told them.

"Did Adam talk about personal things? A vacation or a trip? Where he went to school? Where he grew up?" Nell questioned.

Ed blinked a few times. "Let's see ... he talked about projects he was doing around the house."

"Did he talk about his dog?"

"I don't recall hearing about a dog. Maybe it slipped my mind."

"What about at holiday time? Did Adam tell you anything about his plans? Who he was going to be with?"

"I don't think he said much about it." Lines creased Ed's forehead. "I think he told me he was having a quiet celebration."

Nell began to believe that Ed Barnes either talked the whole time when he was with someone or Adam Timson kept his life very private. "Where was Adam from? Did he grow up around here?"

"Ah, let me think." Ed scratched his head. "I'm not sure Adam mentioned where he was from. At least, I don't remember hearing where he grew up."

"Does Adam speak with an accent? A Boston accent? A Southern accent?"

"No, he doesn't. He doesn't seem to have any accent at all. The way he talks is very generic." Ed shrugged a shoulder. "I'm being no help, am I? I'm ashamed to admit I don't know much about the guy even though I thought I knew him pretty well."

"You *are* a help. You do know things about Adam," Peter reassured him. "Do you happen to know the names of any of Adam's other clients?"

Ed's face brightened. "He does some work for one of the real estate agencies in town, Forward Realty. It's just down the street."

"I need to ask a few difficult questions," Peter informed the man. "Do you know if Adam had any problems with drugs or alcohol?"

Straightening in his seat, Ed said, "Not to my knowledge. He never showed any signs of issues when we got together. Adam was always prepared and professional."

"Do you know if Adam spent any time in prison?"

"Prison? No. I have no idea."

"Had he ever been arrested?"

"Again, I have no idea."

"Does Adam go to church?" Nell asked.

"I think he might attend the Episcopal Church in town, but that might be wrong," Ed said. "I can't say for sure. I don't know where I got that idea."

"Was he involved in any community clubs or boards?"

"I remember he mentioned helping out at the library for some book sale they had. I don't know if volunteering there was a regular thing or not."

"Did Adam talk about having worked for a company or a firm in the past? Did he always do freelance work?" Nell asked.

"I think he's been doing freelance for a long time." Ed swallowed some of his coffee. "That's the impression I got anyway."

AFTER THANKING Ed for his time, Nell and Peter returned to the cruiser and drove away.

"He wasn't a whole lot of help, but at least we know Adam does some work for the realty firm here in town and he doesn't have an accent," Peter said as he merged into traffic.

Nell agreed, and then added, "There are other things we learned, too. Adam is either very private about his personal life or he didn't want to encourage a buddy-buddy relationship with his clients. He behaves professionally and produces quality work. He's done some projects around his house so he must be handy."

"But we don't know where he grew up." Peter recapped some things they'd discussed in the visit. "We don't know if he's been married, if he has kids. It doesn't seem that he was dating, but Adam might not have shared details from his dating life with Ed Barnes."

"There was something I thought was odd." Nell eyed the cloud cover overhead looking for any signs of an approaching storm. "Adam didn't seem to speak to Ed about Oscar. Ed didn't know Adam had a dog. How would that not come up? Oscar seemed to be a big part of Adam's life."

"Like you said, Adam is probably a private person." Peter carefully followed the curves in the road. "He must keep his personal life to himself."

"Do you think Adam might have done something wrong? Something bad?" Nell asked. "Is that why he had to take off so suddenly?"

"Anything is possible. The guy could be off on

some pleasure trip and has no clue the police have concerns about him. On the other side of it, Adam could very well have done something bad and took off before anyone found out about it. He could be halfway around the world by now."

"I wonder." Nell rubbed at her eyes. "Could we go back to Adam's house?"

Peter gave Nell a quick glance. "For what?"

"I want to look through his trash."

7

By the time Nell and Peter arrived, Violet was sitting in her car in Adam Timson's driveway waiting for them. Nell had called her sister and asked if she could meet them. One of their part-time workers was glad to stay longer working in the shop and the employee told Violet it was fine with her if she needed to leave.

When the three of them got out of the cars, Nell and Peter gave Violet an update from their meeting with Ed Barnes.

"You learned a few things," Violet told them. "It was good you met with him. So why did you ask me to meet you here?"

"I need you to help me," Nell admitted.

Violet gave her sister the eye. "With what?"

J. A. WHITING

"I want to go through Adam's trash."

Even though her eyes widened, Violet's face remained neutral. "What do you really want me to help with?"

"That's it. The trash."

"Why?" Violet scrunched up her face in distaste.

Peter said, "We want to see if there's anything from the trash that can give us a clue as to where Adam went."

Violet groaned, but then thought of something that might get her out of the nasty task. "You can't go back in Adam's house. Law enforcement has no reason to enter the home."

Nell pointed to the end of the driveway where a large trash receptacle stood. "Adam must have put the trash out right before he left. He didn't want the house stinking with unemptied trash left inside. We're hoping the garbage truck hasn't come by yet."

"It's been days. The truck must have come by now." Violet looked relieved that she'd probably escaped the trash picking task.

"It hasn't been a week yet and that trash bin looks undisturbed," Nell said. "I bet Adam's trash gets picked up tomorrow or the day after that. Let's go have a look."

Violet sighed. "I'm crossing my fingers that the

thing is empty. I should have asked what crazy idea you had when you called me. I'm making a mental note to myself to always ask what you have in mind before I agree to it."

Peter swung back the large black cover. "It's full."

A groan escaped Violet's throat. "I think I have an appointment I forgot about."

"Nice try." Nell took her sister's arm. "Peter has pairs of surgical-type gloves for all of us. It won't be so bad."

"Does he have a clothespin for my nose so I don't have to inhale the nasty smells?"

Nell chuckled.

In the side yard away from the neighbors' view, Peter pulled out the trash bags, opened one, and dumped the contents onto the grass.

"Great. Just great." Violet tugged the gloves onto her hands and scrunched up her nose. "What are we looking for?"

"Anything that might tell us where Adam went or what caused him to leave so hastily." Nell knelt down to begin combing through the pile of trash.

Peter opened two more bags and dumped them out. "Here's a pile for you," he told Violet.

They started picking through the trash piles

sorting out papers and bills. Violet sat on the brick walkway to look more carefully at the items.

"Look at this." Nell walked over to the other two and held out a withdrawal slip from a bank. "Look at the amount Adam took out of his account."

Peter's eyes bugged out of his head. "Fifteen thousand dollars?"

"I guess Adam's planning to be away for a while," Nell deadpanned.

While Peter took out his phone to make a call to Chief Lambert, Nell and Violet continued to poke through the debris.

"That's it." Nell glanced disappointedly at the trash they'd finished going through.

"The withdrawal slip was a great find," Violet pointed out. "Now we know the bank Adam uses and we know he made a big withdrawal. What was the date on the bank slip?"

"The morning before he left." When Nell poked the trash with her toe, she noticed a store receipt and nonchalantly picked it up. Her heart rate sped up when she read what was on it. "Look at this."

Violet said, "He made a shopping trip to the store. So?"

"It was the same morning he went to the bank. Take a look at the purchases he made."

Peter came over to see what they were looking at.

"Eyebrow gel, an eyebrow pencil."

"What are those things?" Peter questioned.

"Women use them to darken or emphasize their eyebrows," Violet explained.

Peter's forehead scrunched. "Why?"

"To make them look nice. It's part of a makeup routine."

Peter still looked confused.

"Keep reading," Nell encouraged.

"A pair of eyeglasses, a baseball hat." Violet's eyebrows shot up. "Dark brown hair dye."

"Really?" Peter asked with an astonished tone.

"Those things sure sound like ways to camouflage your looks, don't they?" Nell asked.

"THERE'S nothing illegal about changing or enhancing your appearance," Nell said as she and her friend slowed to a walk after completing a four-mile run.

"Maybe not," Dr. Rob Jennette said. "But the reason you're changing the way you look might be related to something illegal. This guy might have committed a crime and decided to run from the police or he's gone somewhere with the intention of committing a crime. And before he took off, he *enhanced* his appearance. It's suspicious."

Thirty-five-years old with dark brown hair and brown eyes, Rob was slim and just under six feet tall. The doctor had met Nell more than ten years ago when she consented to be tested to confirm earlier examinations about her visual abilities, and over the years, as he worked with her to understand her skills, the two had become good friends.

A month ago, Rob had arrived on Nell's doorstep with a bouquet of flowers for her shortly after she'd been involved in uncovering the identity of a killer. For a moment, something seemed to pass between them that felt like a whole lot more than friendship, but the sensation was brief and nothing more came of it as they maintained the *friend* status of their relationship.

"It's a weird case." Nell wiped some perspiration from her brow. "I don't know what to think about Adam."

"You saw colors in his home and on the dog," Rob said. "The colors could be from the man's emotions of fear or worry, or they could be the result of the man's rage about something. He's changing his appearance either because he's afraid of something or because he wants to do something wrong."

Nell tugged the elastic from her ponytail and her auburn hair fell softly just below her shoulders. "If Adam is afraid of something, why doesn't he go to the police for help?"

"Good question."

Rob and Nell returned to the campus of the hospital and medical school where Rob worked as an ophthalmologist seeing patients and doing research. He'd suggested to Nell that they set up an experiment to test her abilities in seeing the colors being emitted by people. In her twenty-seven years of life, she'd never had the experience of seeing people's emotions as colors until a month ago. Rob suspected the change in her visual skill came about from living through the traumatic event of the tornado.

Rob's theory was that emotional energy was like the radiation wavelengths of the visible spectrum, and that Nell was able to pick up on that energy and see it as different colors. Tetrachromats had four types of cones in their eyes instead of the usual three kinds. The cones are structures in the eye that are adjusted to absorb certain wavelengths of light. Rob speculated that the extra cone in Nell's eyes could be giving her the capability to perceive more dimensions of energy … energy from people's emotions that could be visible to a tetrachromat.

"How involved will you be with this investigation?" Rob asked his friend.

"I'll do whatever Chief Lambert thinks I can help with."

"The last case almost got you killed." Rob's brown eyes darkened. "You're not trained in law enforcement. You shouldn't be put in harm's way."

"The chief doesn't put me in harm's way," Nell protested. "I sit in on interviews. I come up with ideas based on the colors I see. The guy replacing our deck happened to be the killer in that last case. How likely is that to ever happen again?"

"It only needs to happen once to get you killed. I really don't want to lose a friend."

Nell was surprised that Rob was going on about her safety. "I'll be okay."

They walked out of the university snack bar with containers of yogurt and bottles of water and went to the patio to sit at the umbrella tables. Pots of flowers had been set around the space making it a pretty place to sit and eat.

"Have you considered taking a self-defense

class?" Rob asked. "The university has a session coming up. Why don't you and Violet sign up?"

"I'll talk to her about it. Why don't you send me the information."

"Really? You'll think about it?" Rob opened his container of water.

"Yes, of course." Nell eyed him playfully. "I'm not that stubborn you know."

"Oh, is that so?" Rob rolled his eyes and laughed. "Then there must be a different Nell Finley I know."

Nell grinned. "No, I think I'm the right one."

"Yeah." Rob returned her smile. "I think you are."

8

Oscar and Iris snoozed on the rugs in Nell's studio at the back of the shop she owned with Violet. Big windows let the light flood the room, the walls were painted white, and the floors were glossy wood.

Nell sat at an easel painting a seascape from some photographs she had pinned to the bulletin board next to her. The painting was a riot of colors ... the ocean sparkled with blues, violets, and light greens, and the foam on the crashing waves shone white and gold and silver. It looked like an impressionistic interpretation and its wild array of colors seemed to have come from a fantasy ... only to Nell, this was the way she saw the world. Actually, the shades and hues Nell could see far exceeded what showed in the painting because her paints, even when mixed, were much too limited to capture what was visible to her.

Placing her brushes on the table, Nell leaned back to stretch the muscles in her back. She'd been painting for hours and was pleased with the progress. She was also happy that she hadn't once thought about Adam Timson during the creative session. It was a relief to get lost in the work and let the analytical part of her mind relax for a while.

Oscar stood up and walked over to Nell. He put his head in her lap hoping she'd scratch behind his ears, and she obliged the sweet, easygoing dog.

"What a good boy," she cooed to him.

Iris lifted her head and tapped her tail on the floor, and Nell looked over at her. "And you're the best girl dog there is." Iris almost seemed to smile from the praise.

Violet came into the backroom from the retail part of the store where she'd been arranging some new pottery pieces she'd recently made. "You want to take a break? How about some lunch?"

"I'd love some lunch."

The sisters had a small refrigerator and a microwave tucked into one of the corners of the room so when they were working, they didn't have to go into the main part of the house to get food or drinks.

Violet made two salads while Nell heated some tomato bisque soup in the microwave, and when it was ready, the sisters carried their lunch to the small table set by the windows overlooking the side yard.

"The gardens really look great now." Violet admired the flower beds edged around the green lawn. "I was worried we wouldn't be able to get them looking like Mom had them, but we've done a decent job."

"I think we'll get better at gardening as we go along. Maybe we inherited Mom's green thumb."

Violet smiled as she raised her spoon to her lips. "I wouldn't go that far, but what we lack in talent, we make up with hard work."

"Sometimes, I think about how strange it is to be in the house without Mom here with us," Nell said. "Once in a while, I think I hear her footsteps and almost call to her to come see a painting I'm working on."

"She was your biggest fan," Violet said. "Besides me."

"We're lucky we have each other." Nell nodded at her sister.

"We sure are." Violet's smile faded a little. "When

I think about Adam Timson, I can't help but feel badly for him. He seems to be all alone. No family we know of, no wife or partner, he works for himself with no colleagues to talk with. Does he have any friends? It seems like a very lonely existence. At least he had Oscar for company."

"I wonder why he lived that way?" Nell placed her fork on her plate. "Was he shy? Had he been hurt by someone and didn't want to take a chance on love anymore?"

"Adam's client didn't indicate to you that Adam was odd or cold or unfriendly," Violet pointed out. "So why be so alone in the world?"

"Maybe the police just haven't found his friends yet." Nell tried to sound hopeful. "He must have had a friend or two. I wish we could ask Oscar some questions."

"I bet that dog knows a whole bunch of stuff that would help the police. If only he could talk." Violet looked over at Oscar and he thumped his tail.

"I guess I'd better get ready. Peter will be picking me up in a little while."

"Good luck this afternoon," Violet said encouragingly. "I bet you'll learn something about Adam from the people at the bank."

PETER AND NELL sat in the bank manager's office. Marcy Dollar was in her fifties, carried a little extra weight and had short, stylish blond hair.

Nell smiled inwardly at the manager's last name. It must have been her destiny to work in a financial institution.

"I don't know Mr. Timson well," Marcy said. "I'm familiar with him coming into the bank. I've spoken with him briefly. He's always soft-spoken and polite."

"We understand Adam made a large withdrawal the other day," Peter said.

The manager's eyebrows raised in surprise that the police officer knew that Adam had withdrawn money recently. "You understand that a client's financial status is confidential?"

"I do. We know how much Adam took out of his account. Could you tell me if he was given his money in cash?" Peter asked. "Would that be a breach of confidence?"

Marcy moved around in her seat and seemed to be wrestling with what to say. She chose her words carefully when she spoke. "I'm not sure, but I believe he did not receive a bank check."

So he did take his withdrawal in cash. Nell was

impressed with the manager's cleverly worded sentence. Marcy had not mentioned Adam's name when she answered and did not specifically say he received cash.

"Do you know where Adam lived prior to buying his house here in town?" Peter questioned.

"He lived in a short-term apartment over on Woodland Street." She pulled up some online information from her computer. "Mr. Timson lived in the apartment for a year before buying his house. Prior to that, he lived in an apartment in Worcester, Massachusetts for four years."

Nell had to keep her expression even when she heard the name of the city where Adam had previously lived. She and Violet had grown up in Worcester, and that's where Nell was when the tornado roared through. Adam must have moved away from Worcester about a year and half before they did. *Lucky him. He avoided that tornado.*

The manager said, "I do recall Adam telling me he always wanted to live by the ocean and that was why he moved here."

"Do you know anything about his family?" Peter asked.

Marcy said, "I don't remember him mentioning

any family members. His name is the only one on the mortgage."

"Did he give you an emergency contact?"

"No, it wasn't necessary. We never asked for that sort of information."

When there wasn't anything more to discuss, Peter and Nell left the bank and stepped out into the sunshine, but before they could walk to the car, a woman came out of the bank.

"Excuse me." The woman looked to be in her late-thirties, was petite and slim, had shoulder-length light brown hair and big blue eyes. Nell recognized her as a teller who'd been working at the bank counter. "I heard you asking about Adam Timson."

"Do you know Adam?" Peter asked.

"Not well. We make small talk whenever he comes into the bank." The woman looked back to the building. "He's a nice guy, he seems kind. I heard that he disappeared."

"Not exactly disappeared. Adam left town for a while," Peter explained. "We'd like to locate him. Would you happen to know where he might have gone?"

"Why do you want to talk to him?"

"We found his dog." Nell smiled at the teller trying to make her feel more at ease.

"Oh, is that all?" The teller smiled, too. "I thought something bad had happened."

"We don't want Adam to worry about the dog and we'd like to know when he's coming back," Nell said. "I'm taking care of the dog until we can locate Adam."

"That's very nice of you."

Nell and Peter introduced themselves.

"I'm Bonnie Plant."

"Do you know any of Adam's friends?" Peter questioned. "We're trying to find someone who knows him well, someone who knows how to contact him."

"Does the manager have his phone number listed on his documents? Did you ask her?"

"We have Adam's phone number," Peter informed her. "But he's not picking up. It might be an old number."

"I see. Too bad. I don't know any of his friends, but I did see him at a pub in town one night. He was with Mike Forward. Mike owns Forward Realty here in town."

"When was this?" Peter asked.

"Maybe a month ago?" Bonnie guessed. "I went

out for drinks with a friend. She wasn't feeling well and left before I did. I was finishing my drink when Adam saw me and came over. We talked for a little while before Mike showed up."

"How did Adam seem? Was he in a good mood? Did he mention an upcoming trip?"

"He was nice, he's always nice," Bonnie said. "He didn't say anything about going away."

"Do you know where Adam lived before he moved here?" Nell asked. "Do you know where he grew up?"

"He lived in Worcester for a few years, I know that. I don't know where he lived when he was young."

"Did Adam mention any family?"

Bonnie's facial muscles tightened. She looked at Peter with worried eyes and then shifted her attention to Nell. "This isn't just about the dog, is it?"

9

Nell and Violet sat at a table in the popular coffee, breakfast, and lunch shop owned by their good friend, Dani. The sun had barely been up for an hour yet the place was abuzz with the early morning customers. The sisters enjoyed coming in once or twice a week before their own shop opened later in the morning.

Enjoying her scrambled eggs and toast, Nell answered questions about her and Peter's visit to the bank.

"Why do you think the teller waited until you were outside before speaking to you about Adam?" Violet sipped from her steaming mug of coffee.

"Bonnie probably didn't want her colleagues or the bank customers to hear her concerns about

Adam." Nell buttered a piece of her toast. "She didn't say anything about it, but I got the impression Bonnie likes Adam."

"Meaning ... she's interested in him romantically?"

"I think she might be. She kept saying what a nice person he is."

"What if Adam turns out to be a criminal? Bonnie's image of Adam is going to be crushed," Violet pointed out. "Did she give you the idea she might have dated Adam?"

"She didn't say anything like that, but if she and Adam haven't dated, I'm pretty sure Bonnie would be happy to go out with him." Nell looked up from her breakfast plate to see Dani coming over to the table.

"I have five minutes to sit down. This place is crazy today."

"It's crazy every day in here," Nell said with a smile. "Haven't you noticed?"

Dani pulled a little corner from Nell's slice of toast and popped it into her mouth. "I'm starving."

"Do you take food from your other customers' plates?" Nell gave her friend a look.

"Just from you. You're very lucky." When Dani smiled, her perfect white teeth sparkled under the café lights. The young woman was tall and athletic, and had been a star track and field competitor for her university. In her late twenties, she had brown eyes and long, blond hair she wore up in a bun or in a simple braid while she was working. "Peter tells me this case he's working on is a weird one."

"It is. No one can figure out if the guy has innocently gone off on a trip or if he's in some kind of trouble," Violet reported.

"The dog is the thing that bothers me," Dani said checking to see if the takeout counter had become too busy. "The guy must be a rat if he deliberately dumped his dog at the park. How's Oscar doing?"

"He's an angel," Nell told their friend. "He fits right in with us and Iris. We'd be glad to keep him if Adam doesn't want a dog around anymore. I've become attached to Oscar. I hope he'll stay."

"He's a sweetheart," Violet chimed in. "Oscar and Iris are like brother and sister now."

"Do you have any ideas about what's going on? Do you expect the guy to show up back at his house soon?" Dani reached for Nell's buttered toast.

Nell answered slowly. "No. I don't think that's how this will end."

Violet's eyes filled with fear. "How *do* you think it's going to end?"

"Probably not the way we hope it will," Nell said softly.

"Oh, man." Dani had a look of apprehension on her face. "Is this mess something you should back away from?"

"Who knows?" Nell asked with a near groan. "I think Adam is in some kind of trouble. Big trouble."

"I'd like Peter to get assigned to a different case." Dani's voice shook with worry, and then she said quietly, "Do you think the guy is dead?"

Violet squared her shoulders. "I hope he's not dead."

"What do you think got him into trouble?" Dani asked.

Nell shook her head and picked at her eggs. "We don't know. No one has shined a harsh light on Adam. Everyone tells us he's a nice guy."

When Dani looked to the counter again, she stood. "I need to get back to work. I can't sit around all morning like some people can."

Nell chuckled.

"Do you want me to bring you some more toast?" Dani asked.

"No. Thanks anyway." Nell smiled at her friend.

"Too bad you didn't get much of it." Dani said

with an impish grin, and then hurried back to wait on customers.

"Do *you* think Adam's dead?" Violet asked her sister.

Nell glanced out the window at the town coming to life. A number of people were window shopping, some carried takeout cups of coffee, others were taking pictures of the quaint Main Street.

"Nell?"

Nell turned back to her sister. "I don't think he's dead, but I worry he might end up that way."

"Do you think he did wrong? Do you think he committed a crime?"

"When we were in Adam's house the other day, most of the colors in the rooms were normal. The colors were what I expected to see. But in that one room, the kitchen, it was overwhelming. The colors were garish, almost pulsing and bright like a neon sign. There were a lot of emotions left behind in there, but I can't sort them out. Is Adam the aggressor in something? Is he a victim? Whatever he is, he's not just away on a vacation."

"It's a weird coincidence that Adam lived in Worcester before moving to this area," Nell said. "We lived only a few miles away from him for a few years.

He moved to the North Shore about a year before Mom died."

Nell sighed. "And lucky for him, he missed the tornado."

Violet gave her sister a smile. "You're doing much better now with storms."

"I'm doing a *little* better, not *much* better."

"But you're making progress. That's what counts."

Violet's and Nell's phones buzzed at almost the same time.

"It's from John. Look at Iris and Oscar." Nell smiled at the photo their neighbor, John, had sent them. It showed the two dogs lounging on the front porch next to John's wife, Ida. The couple, in their seventies, had been friends of the sisters' parents and had known Nell and Violet for years. When the young women went out or to work, the dogs would often go over to visit John and Ida and enjoyed spending part of the day with them.

Nell looked up. "You know what? Something just occurred to me about Adam Timson's house."

Violet tilted her head to the side in question. "What about it?"

"When we walked through the place with Peter, did you happen to notice the lack of something?"

With narrowed eyes, Violet thought back to being in the house. "I can't think of anything. What was missing?"

"There weren't any pictures in there. I don't recall seeing any photographs. Not a single photo of anyone, not even the dog. It's unusual, isn't it? Most people have a few pictures around the house of the family, or a shot of the owner with a partner or spouse, of their kids, or some photos from a trip, or from walking in the woods, or some landscape photographs from a place they like. I don't remember one single photo in that house."

"I don't know. I don't remember any pictures, but I wasn't paying attention to things like that."

"Doesn't Adam have one picture of someone or something he'd like to display?" Suddenly, flashes of colors sparked in Nell's brain and she had to close her eyes for a few seconds.

"Are you okay?" Violet became alarmed. "What's wrong? Do you have a headache? Can I get you something? Want a glass of cold water?"

"No, I'm okay." Nell's voice was soft and hard to hear amongst the din of the busy café. "Colors were flashing in my head, but they stopped. They're gone now."

"Why did that happen?" Violet questioned her sister.

Nell shrugged and gave a weak smile.

"Do the color flashes have something to do with what we were talking about?"

"Maybe I just need a break from thinking about the case." Nell's hand shook when she reached for her mug of coffee. After taking a swallow of the warm liquid, she set down the mug and looked across the table at her sister. "Why wouldn't anyone display a few photographs? What would be the reason?"

"Maybe all his pictures are on his phone and he's too lazy to print some out and frame them," Violet suggested.

"Okay. I can see that. Are there other reasons?"

"He doesn't like clutter."

"That would fit," Nell said. "The place was kept very neat."

Violet came up with another thought. "When Peter opened the closets in that house, there weren't a lot of things in them. Our closets are stuffed to the breaking point. A lot of the stuff in my closet I don't even wear anymore, but things accumulate. Nothing had accumulated in Adam's closets."

"He might have gotten rid of a bunch of things

when he moved into the house. That's a time when people throw things out," Nell said.

"We moved to our Bluewater house not long ago," Violet said. "And our closets are still full."

"Maybe Adam is the type of person who needs things neat and orderly."

"What's that like?" Violet joked causing her sister to chuckle.

"I don't think we'll ever find out." Finishing off her beverage, Nell took out her wallet. "No photos and uncluttered closets tell us a few things about Adam Timson's personality."

"He's obsessive?" Violet asked.

"Maybe. He even took out the trash and brought the garbage can to the curb before he took off. His neighbor said Adam seemed to be in a hurry, but the guy still took the time to put the trash out."

"Okay then. Definitely obsessive."

"Why did Adam take the time to remove all of the dog's things from the house before leaving?" Nell leaned forward. "And then throw them in a dumpster?"

"No clue. Do you have an answer?" Violet asked.

Nell gave a slight shake of her head. "I wish I did."

10

ike Forward owned the real estate firm in Saxonwood that bore his name. The man was in his mid-forties, had broad shoulders and a medium build. His salt and pepper hair was cut shorter and he had a trimmed beard.

The three of them sat in the corner of the pub where the teller, Bonnie Plant, had talked with Adam about a month ago before Mike arrived that night to have a drink with him.

The pub had a cozy atmosphere with polished wood on the walls, a fireplace on one side, leather booths, a glossy granite bar, and tables and chairs placed around the room.

"Has there been any word about Adam?" Mike asked, concern written all over his face.

"Nothing yet," Peter used a light tone to diminish the man's worry. "I'm sure we'll hear from him soon. He's probably somewhere remote and doesn't even know we're trying to contact him."

"I hope so." Mike wrapped his hand around his beer glass.

"How did you meet Adam?" Peter asked.

"I sold him his house. I found out he did websites and design work so I hired him to do some things for me. Adam is really talented and he actually listens which is rare. He has an easy way about him and he's able to communicate very well why something in a design looks great or doesn't hit the mark."

"The two of you socialized?"

"We came here for drinks or dinner maybe once a month or once every couple of months."

"Did you do anything else together? Golf?" Peter asked.

"No golf. Adam didn't play. I asked him to go to some baseball and football games, but he always declined so I stopped inviting him."

"He wasn't interested in sports?" Nell asked.

"He liked sports just fine. He came to my house a few times to watch a game with me."

"Did he say why he didn't have an interest in attending a game?"

Mike shrugged his shoulder. "Adam said he didn't like crowds. He didn't feel comfortable around a ton of people."

"We've heard Adam is a quiet person. Is that your experience with him?"

"Quiet? Sure, I guess so. We've had some good conversations. He doesn't just sit there and expect you to do all the talking. Adam converses like anyone else. Maybe he prefers small groups to large gatherings ... and since he doesn't like going to stadiums or arenas, it would make sense."

"What do you talk about when you're together?" Peter asked.

"Current events, sports, cars. I enjoy woodworking so I tell him about my projects."

"Does Adam have any hobbies?"

"Adam likes to read. He likes movies. He enjoys walking in the woods."

"Does he have any pets?" Nell asked.

Mike cocked his head. "Pets? I don't think so."

"Have you ever visited Adam's home?"

Mike scrunched up his forehead. "I guess not.

Not socially. I was in the house with him when he was interested in buying it, but no, he always comes to my place or we come here."

"Do you know anything about Adam's past?" Peter questioned. "About his relatives? Where he grew up?"

Mike sat quietly for several moments. "I know he lived in Worcester. I don't know why, but I had the impression Adam grew up there. Once he mentioned he had a sister, but I don't know her name. He didn't talk about her. Do you think he went off for a while to visit her?"

"It's possible." Peter nodded. "What about a girl-friend? Did he date?"

"Not my knowledge. He didn't talk about women. He never told me he was dating." Mike leaned slightly closer. "I had the idea Adam was divorced and didn't want to talk about it."

"Did he mention a past marriage?" Nell asked.

Mike looked a little confused. "No, he didn't. I just got the feeling he'd been married before and it didn't work out. I never brought it up."

"Does Adam talk about any kids he has?"

"I don't think he has any kids. He certainly never talks about kids."

"Do you happen to know where Adam went to school?"

Mike drank from his beer glass. "I'm realizing that I don't know a heck of a lot about Adam. We just never talked about some things. They never came up. I have no idea where he went to school. He never mentioned it to me and I never asked."

"Was Adam involved in any community activities?" Nell asked the man.

"Are you looking for anything specific?"

Nell gave the man a smile. "No. I'm only wondering if Adam enjoyed working with charities or some of the town organizations."

"Maybe he supported some charities privately. It wouldn't surprise me. But Adam never talked about it with me."

"Do you have any pictures of you and Adam together?" Nell was thinking about how Adam's home was devoid of any photographs.

"Uh. I don't think I do."

"Can you tell us what Adam was like?"

"Oh, sure. He was a good listener, good to talk to. He seemed like a kind person, easygoing. Adam kept in shape, worked out, did some running. He loved watching baseball, loved being outside. He was a computer whiz. He could fix anything that was wrong with my computers. He did a great website for me and lots of terrific ads and graphic design work." Mike looked pleased that he was finally able to answer a question in detail.

"Adam worked out?" Peter asked. "Do you know the name of the gym he went to?"

Mike said, "Oh, no, he didn't go to a gym. He worked out at home. Adam told me he really didn't need any equipment, he used what was around the house, used his own bodyweight. The guy was frugal. He didn't want to spend money on a gym when he was able to work out at home for free."

"He was a runner?" Nell asked.

"Six days a week. Adam runs on the state park trails." Mike smiled. "He tried his best to get me to run with him, but there is absolutely no way I'm going jogging. It's either too hot or humid, too cold, too windy, too rainy, too snowy. Nope. I have certain standards. Running is not for me. I leave that foolishness to Adam, and he's welcome to it."

Nell chuckled. "That's a very good argument against running."

"Do you run?" Mike asked.

"A little. My sister is an excellent runner."

"Don't get sucked into your sister's lunacy. Those

kinds of people aren't normal. Normal people don't enjoy that sort of foolishness."

The man's comments made Nell smile.

"When you go out for drinks together, does Adam drink a lot?" Peter asked.

"No, he never gets drunk. Two beers, that's his limit. He told me drinking more than two will ruin his workouts."

"Is there anything else you can tell us about Adam?" Peter asked.

Mike took in a long breath and thought it over. "I was just thinking ... Adam is a great guy, but I don't know much about him. I never realized how little we talk about ourselves, how few questions we ask about each other. It's almost like we're being secretive. We aren't, of course. I suppose it's just the way a lot of guys socialize."

IT WAS dark outside when Nell and Peter returned to his car. Peter didn't want to take the cruiser to the pub so as not to attract attention that a police officer was there asking questions.

Nell shut the passenger side door and snapped in her seatbelt. "Do you and your friends talk about yourselves when you're together? Do you ask each other personal questions?"

As he drove out of the pub's parking lot, Peter looked horrified. "What kinds of personal questions?"

"Simple things like where you grew up, where you went to school. The kinds of questions we asked Mike Forward about Adam."

"Oh. My friends know where we grew up because we all grew up around here."

"You know what I mean," Nell told him. "Do you only talk about sports and working out or food or music? Do you ever share your feelings? If you're feeling bad about something, do you tell your friends what's going on?"

"No. Guys don't do that."

"Some guys do," Nell said. "It's healthy to do that. And, if Mike and Adam had done that, we'd have a lot more information than we have right now."

"It wasn't a total loss," Peter said. "We learned that Adam doesn't drink much."

"And that he doesn't like crowds," Nell added. "Why doesn't Adam tell his friends he has a dog? Why doesn't Adam invite Mike to his house? Why does he only meet Mike at the pub or at Mike's house?"

"Some people don't like to entertain. They don't like to prepare food, they don't like the mess in their house, they don't want to have to clean up. You pointed out to me that Adam is really picky about clutter. He likes things just so. I can see someone with that kind of personality not wanting to enter-tain." Peter took a right turn and headed the car towards Bluewater Cove. "Did you notice any colors on Mike? Was he giving off any emotions in colors?"

"The only thing I saw was light-red orange which I'm learning seems to represent concern and worry, or disappointment or shame. I'm becoming aware that certain shades of colors have subtle meanings, like all shades of red don't stand for one thing. They suggest different emotions even though they're in the same color family."

"So Mike was giving off feelings of concern?" Peter asked.

"Yes, and when he admitted not knowing much about Adam, he gave off a different shade of red that I'm figuring out means feeling bad about something ... like when you disappoint someone and feel bad about it."

When they stopped at a red light, Peter's phone buzzed and he put it to his ear, listening. "Okay. I'm not far away. I'm on it." He pulled the car to the right and made a U-turn. "We have to make a detour before we head back. There's a problem at Adam Timson's house."

Nell turned in her seat, her heart beginning to race. "What kind of a problem?"

"Gunshots reported." Peter stomped on the gas pedal and the car sped down the road.

11

Nell and Peter didn't say much to each other on the short ride to Adam Timson's house. When they arrived, there was an ambulance and several police cars parked near the driveway with their blue lights flashing.

"Stay in the car," Peter said before getting out and striding over to the other officers.

Nell didn't want to wait in the car. Her skin felt like pins and needles and she wanted to know what had happened to cause such a commotion. Peering through the windshield, she spotted Chief Lambert speaking with two officers. Once things calmed down, she hoped it would be safe for her to leave the vehicle, but for now, she put her window down to try and hear what was going on.

After fifteen minutes passed, the chief approached the car and waved to Nell indicating she should come out.

"Would you prefer to stay in the car?" the chief asked.

"No, I've been dying to get out of there." Nell looked towards Adam's house. "Did Adam come back?"

"No, he didn't." Chief Lambert started for the driveway. "Walk with me. The neighbors were sitting in the family room at the back of their house."

"Sheryl and Scott McKenzie?"

"That's right. They saw a light come on in Adam's place and then go off. Because the light went out so quickly, the couple worried either Adam had returned and might be injured or unwell, or there was an intruder in the home. Scott called Adam's number, but there was no answer so he decided to go over to investigate."

"Oh, no." Nell was sure Scott must have been shot by the intruder.

As Nell and the chief were going up the driveway, the emergency medical personnel came around the back of the house with a stretcher carrying Scott.

The man rested quietly on his back with his eyes closed.

"Is he going to be okay?" Nell asked as the stretcher was whisked away to the waiting ambulance.

"He suffered a gunshot wound to the right side of the chest. An officer told me one of the EMTs expects him to make it."

Nell was stunned watching Scott McKenzie get loaded into the ambulance. "Where's his wife?"

"She's inside with an EMT. She passed out. She heard the gunshot, called the police, and rushed over here to find Scott inside the garage on his back," Chief Lambert explained. "Sheryl will be taken to the hospital as soon as she's feeling steady."

"Was the intruder caught?"

"Long gone." The chief looked into the garage through the opened doors keeping his eye on the investigators.

Nell followed his gaze and saw the colors floating like ribbons on the air. "I'd guess nobody saw anything when this happened. Have there been any break-ins around here? In this part of town?"

"No one saw anything. This isn't my jurisdiction, but the Saxonwood Chief of Police was good enough to call and involve us. Would you be comfortable going inside?"

"Um." Nell glanced warily at the house. "I guess I would."

"I'd like you to go in with me and look around. Don't touch anything. We'll walk through the first floor and then come back out. We won't go into the garage where the man was shot. How does that sound?"

"There are colors in the garage," Nell informed the chief. "They're kind of hanging heavy in the air."

"What do you see?"

"Black. Reds. Orange. Different shades. The colors are floating on the air like wavy streaks of dust particles."

"What does it mean?"

"It symbolizes fear, death, anger, and something else I don't understand. The colors look different than usual. They're more transparent, dull." Nell gave a helpless shrug. "I haven't seen this before."

"Okay. That's interesting." Chief Lambert gave the slightest of nods. "Shall we go inside?"

The house was abuzz with investigators and officers. Peter was near the door to the garage speaking with a plainclothes police officer. All the lights were on and it felt far too bright to Nell. She followed the chief from room to room, moving slowly around the members of law enforcement, until they left the house through the front door.

"Did you see anything in there?" the chief questioned.

"The frame around the door leading out of the kitchen to the rear yard was glowing red. The kitchen walls from the outside door to the garage are pulsing with red. The intruder must have entered the home through the back door. He left his emotions all over that area. Were there signs of forced entry?"

"No. We assume the person had a key or was skilled in picking a lock. If he used a pick, it wasn't the first time he'd done so. The knob and the lock are clean ... no scratches or pick marks are visible."

An awful thought entered Nell's head. "Do you think it was Adam? Did he return home?"

"We're leaning towards thinking it wasn't Adam, but that's conjecture right now."

"Why would the intruder shoot the neighbor?" Nell asked.

The chief said, "Scott McKenzie had the code for the garage. He pressed the numbers and the door went up. It was dark inside. Scott didn't turn on the lights. When he stepped into the garage, the kitchen door opened and there was a flash and a bang. Scott managed to share that much with the first officer on the scene."

"So was someone inside waiting for Adam?" Nell speculated. "The intruder might have thought Adam was coming home and fired on him."

"It's a definite possibility," the chief agreed. "Someone may have come to snoop around looking for clues to where Adam went. He heard the garage door opening and thought it could be Adam returning so he went to the door and shot him."

"Only the victim was the neighbor, not Adam," Nell said. "Was Scott able to give a description of the person who shot him?"

"Scott couldn't see him. It was dark. He only saw the flash of the gun."

"If the shooter wasn't Adam, are you thinking Adam took off because he was afraid of someone? Because he knew someone was going to come looking for him?"

"It's looking like that, isn't it?" the chief said.

"Who is so angry with Adam that he's prepared to kill him?" Nell asked. "What did Adam do to make someone so angry?"

"Those are the million dollar questions."

Violet went to get Nell after she received a phone call to come and pick her up. They returned home and went to the living room to talk about what happened at Adam's house. Iris and Oscar were allowed to snuggle on the sofa with the sisters.

"I wasn't expecting this." Violet shook her head while running her hand over Oscar's soft coat. "It puts a new spin on everything. A dangerous spin."

Nell nervously rattled on about the evening from meeting and talking with Mike Forward from the real estate agency to riding in the car with Peter when the call came in reporting gunshots at Adam Timson's house.

"What could Adam be mixed up in?" Nell asked.

"Whatever it is, the players mean business."

"Mike Forward told us Adam is careful about his alcohol intake and only ever has two beers when they're together. He also said Adam doesn't like crowds and always refused invitations to a sports stadium. Mike has never been to Adam's house. They met at a pub or they went to Mike's place when they got together. After our questions, Mike was surprised when he realized how very little he knew about Adam."

Violet pulled a throw blanket over her legs. "I know this sounds crazy, but doesn't it seem like Adam was expecting something to happen to him? He was careful never to get drunk and not have his wits about him. He didn't want to be in crowds. Was that because there were too many people to keep his eye on?"

Nell nodded. "That's what I wondered. He seems to very carefully control his environment. He works at home. He doesn't have a partner. The neighbors said he didn't seem to go out much, that he spends a lot of time at home. It paints a picture of someone who wants to know who's around him, who doesn't want to take the chance of being too exposed."

"What on earth did Adam do to require such a sheltered, careful, vigilant existence?"

"Whatever it was, he knew someone would come for him eventually." Sound asleep, Iris had her head in Nell's lap and she gently rested her arm over the dog's back.

Violet's eyes widened. "That's why Adam left Oscar in the park. He must have known something was about to happen and he didn't want to put Oscar in danger. Adam knew someone would find the dog and would take him in."

"You're right." Nell patted Iris's head. "Sometimes

I thought badly about Adam for leaving his dog, but now it makes perfect sense. He was trying to protect Oscar."

"From who? Who is this guy with a gun?" Violet asked. "This is serious stuff. Remind me never to go back inside Adam's house ... or in his yard ... or his driveway, or anywhere within a mile of his place. Make that ten miles." Violet looked directly at her sister. "Don't you go back there. Ever."

"What do you think Adam is involved with?" Nell asked.

"Drugs? Gangs? Internet crime? Smuggling? I really don't know. What other kinds of illegal activities are there?"

"Larceny. Assault." Nell's face paled a little. "Murder?"

12

———

The scent of pine trees filled the air as Nell, Violet, Iris, and Oscar walked along the trails in the state park. The dogs ran ahead sniffing the ground and the trees, watched birds fly out of the field grass, and rushed down to the lake and splashed around in the water.

"We're going to have two dirty water rats to drag home after this adventure," Violet laughed at the dogs' antics.

"It's worth it. We all needed this." Nell loved the state park trails, the tall trees shading the paths, the sunlight filtering down through the leaves, the millions of nature's colors harmonizing together so beautifully. It was so different than being in a big store or in a stadium where so many colors were fighting and conflicting with the others. It could make Nell's head spin and bring on terrible headaches. The compatible colors of nature in forests, fields, snowstorms, and at the seaside balanced and coordinated perfectly and filled Nell with tranquility.

"Are you meeting Rob tomorrow?" Violet picked up a little pebble and tried to skip it over the lake.

"We're going to try a casual experiment. Rob found a video of people expressing different emotions in various settings. He wants to use it to see if I can pick up the colors from their emotions. I've been seeing various shades of colors. I think the different shades and hues represent different emotions. Take the color red. There are so many variations to it ... cranberry, magenta, barn red, candy apple, rust, salmon, raspberry. I think each variation can stand for a subtle emotion or characteristic like aggression, violence, fear, anger, passion. I've only tapped the surface of understanding what the colors symbolize."

"You're going to have to carry around a huge binder wherever you go so you can reference what you're seeing," Violet said with a grin.

"When I was at Adam's house the other night, the colors looked strange to me. The reds were pulsing in the air. The blacks looked like long, heavy streamers swelling and surging."

"Those colors get left behind by the person's mood and emotions?" Violet asked. "They linger? The person doesn't need to be present for you to see their feelings?"

"It's like when someone who is wearing perfume walks through a room. They leave the scent behind for a little while. It's still on the air even though the person has left the room," Nell explained.

Violet smiled. "That's a great description. It's an easy way for me to understand how you're seeing the colors. What will Rob do tomorrow? Show you a video clip of something emotional like an argument or someone who's afraid of something and then you'll see the colors and match the shade to the person's emotion?"

"Something like that. We're not sure it will work if I'm watching a film and I'm not in the same actual space with the people. We'll see. Rob is eager to find out if a video or a film can capture emotions in a way that I'll be able to see them as colors."

"It sounds cool. Can I come watch?" Violet asked.

"Sure you can. You always help me feel calm." Nell watched the dogs trot ahead on the winding path. "Rob told me there's going to be a self-defense class at the university. He thinks we should sign up."

"Because we're often in dangerous situations now that you have this special skill?"

"Yup. That's what he said. He worries about us."

"It's probably a good idea for us to do it. You never know when it might come in handy," Violet said.

"We can sign up online when we get home. Rob will be very happy we took his advice," Nell smiled. "You know ... sometimes I feel ... I don't know how to explain it. When I'm with Rob, sometimes I feel like we're flirting with each other."

Violet looked at her sister. "Really? Is this new?"

"Very new. The first time I felt it was a month ago when Rob brought me flowers after I was almost attacked by the killer from the last case. I felt it again when we were sitting together on the medical school's patio after we went running."

"Is something developing between you two?" Violet looked pleased by the possibility.

"We've been friends for years. It would be weird if something changed between us, wouldn't it?" Nell asked.

"No, it would be nice. Go with it and see where it leads."

The sisters joined the dogs at the edge of the large lake, took off their shoes and waded in the cool water while Iris and Oscar chased each other around the sandy perimeter.

"We should have brought swimsuits," Nell said splashing her face and arms to cool off from the late afternoon heat.

"Next time," Violet told her sister. "We should probably head back soon. Emily needs to leave the shop by 5pm."

"Oh, right." Nell called to the dogs.

Iris was lapping at the water, but Oscar was turned away from her looking off into the trees. His gaze was intent as if he saw a squirrel or a rabbit he wanted to chase. Nell called him again not wanting the dog to dart off into the woods.

Oscar turned his head to her, and then turned his attention back to whatever had caught his eye. He whined and sniffed the air.

Violet called Iris and clapped her hands. "Come on, girl. If Iris comes, Oscar will probably follow."

Iris trotted back to where the sisters were standing and was praised for coming to them, but Oscar was riveted by something off behind the trees.

Nell started walking towards him. "I'll get him. We don't have time to chase him through the woods."

When she reached the dog, she patted his head and clipped the leash to his collar. "What are you so interested in? Is there a deer?" Nell followed Oscar's sightline, but couldn't see anything moving beyond the trees. The light was especially beautiful in that area with different shades of yellow and white shining between the branches.

"Come on, good dog. It's time to go home."

Oscar whined and wagged his tail. He didn't want to budge. Something about the situation caused a flutter of nervousness to run over Nell's skin, and she tugged gently on the leash to get the dog moving.

Finally, Oscar began to follow, but every few seconds, he turned his head to look back at the spot in the trees that had taken his attention.

"What was back there?" Violet asked. "A squirrel?"

"I couldn't see anything, but Oscar didn't want to leave."

"I bet it was a rabbit or a deer or something," Violet said.

"Or a bear?" Nell kidded her sister.

"Oh gosh, not a bear." Violet looked over her shoulder. "It better not be a bear that comes out from that thicket. I'd faint dead away. You'd have to carry me out of here."

Nell chuckled at the thought.

"Let's walk faster," Violet urged as she picked up the pace.

SITTING OUTSIDE on the deck of their neighbors' house, Nell and Violet enjoyed the delicious calzones and salad made by John and Ida. Seventy-eight-year-old John was short, spry, and stocky while his seventy-six-year-old Ida was tall and sturdy. They'd both rushed to Nell's aid during the last case she was involved with when the killer entered her kitchen and threatened her.

The evening was warm and pleasant with a clear sky of twinkling stars. Iris and Oscar rested on the deck sniffing the air and watching over the yard.

Nell shared some details of the investigation into the missing man with the neighbors, being careful to avoid anything the police had not yet shared with the public.

"The poor neighbor was being a good Samaritan

going over to check on Mr. Timson's house," John said. "Unfortunately, he was not rewarded for his concern."

"How is Scott McKenzie doing?" Ida asked as she passed around a bottle of wine.

"Scott is out of danger now from the successful surgery," Nell explained. "He'll need to stay in the hospital for a few more days and then they'll allow him to go home."

Ida shook her head. "He is one lucky man."

"He'd have been luckier if he hadn't been shot," John pointed out.

"It's a nasty business." Ida added more salad to her plate. "Was someone looking for Adam or was it a burglar caught in the act of looting Timson's home?"

Nell said, "I'm leaning towards the idea the gunman was looking for Adam."

"No one knows if Timson has family?" John asked. "The man had some friends and clients. Wouldn't you think Timson would have mentioned a relative to one of them?"

"It does seem unusual." Violet lifted a forkful of the calzone to her mouth.

"Do you think he's hiding from something?" Ida

asked. "Or someone? And that's the reason for his reluctance to talk about his background?"

"I think that's a very real possibility." Nell praised the delicious meal. "I don't think it was a random gunman who was in Adam's house. I think the intruder was waiting to see if Adam would return home that night. When he heard the garage door opening, he opened the kitchen door and fired. He was taking no chances. He wanted Adam dead."

"This whole thing reminds me of something I read years ago." John folded his napkin and set it on the table.

"What did you read?" Nell was eager to hear what her neighbor was referring to.

"It was about people in the federal witness protection program. Many of the witnesses were involved in criminal activities themselves, but were placed into protection after they gave key testimony in court. After their testimony, they were given new names and social security numbers, whisked away to a new city or town, and helped with finding employment. Some of the witnesses don't follow the directions they're given, and end up getting killed. The article reported that witnesses have to be very careful to lay low, live quietly, not draw attention to themselves. They have to check-in with the federal marshals once a year. This man, Timson, sounds like he lived the way the witnesses were supposed to."

Nell's heart began to race. *Was Adam Timson in witness protection?*

13

Nell and Violet chattered at Rob while he was setting up the video equipment and the screen.

"John Patrick wonders if Adam Timson is in witness protection," Nell said causing Rob to stop what he was doing and stare at her.

"Witness protection? Then why did he take off?" Rob had a puzzled expression on his face. "Wait a minute. Who is in charge of people in protection?"

"Federal marshals," Violet told him.

"So if federal marshals got wind that someone was planning to go after Timson, they may have swooped in and taken him away," Rob speculated.

"It makes sense, doesn't it?" Nell asked.

"Someone was at Adam's house with a gun and shot the neighbor thinking it was Adam returning home."

"It does make sense." Rob nodded.

"That's why Adam took the dog and left him at the park. Adam got rid of all the dog's things ... food, bowls, leash. He didn't want the people who were after him to hurt Oscar."

Nell said, "And that's why Adam didn't keep any photos around the house and why he had few belongings, and didn't invite people to his place. He was living carefully, trying to fly under the radar. If his few friends and associates didn't know much about Adam, they couldn't spill information to someone who came looking for him."

"It makes perfect sense." Rob returned to setting up the video equipment.

"It also makes sense that Adam bought hair dye, glasses, makeup, and a hat," Nell pointed out. "He's trying to disguise himself."

"Have you told the police about your idea?" Rob questioned.

"Not yet. We'll tell them today." Nell sat down in the chair that had been placed close to the screen.

Rob finished the set-up. "I'm going to show you the first scenario. Let's see if any colors come off the people during their interaction."

"Where did you get these films?" Violet asked.

"They're often used to teach social skills. Some of them are from classes on self-defense showing some dangerous situations and what you should do to get out of them."

"Okay. I'm ready." Nell moved a little in the chair to get comfortable.

Rob turned off the lights and pressed the button for the first filmed situation to play and the screen filled with images of middle school students milling around the front of a school waiting for the morning bell.

A small, thin boy was off to the side looking timid and quiet. A group of three boys approached wearing smug smiles. They began to pick at the boy, at first, verbally bullying him, until one of them pushed the boy and knocked off his backpack. One of the others kicked the frightened youngster. Other students standing around turned and walked away.

Rob stopped the video and flipped on the lights.

"That enraged me," Nell said, her hands folded into fists. "Nobody helped that kid. They all let those jerks bully him. I really don't like the word *bullying*, it's too weak. It's too easy to dismiss. Bullying is a form of assault and should be called what it is." Nell went on for another minute ranting about the treatment the middle schooler had to endure.

"Did you see any colors?" Rob asked.

"What?" Nell blinked at him and pushed her auburn hair off her shoulders. "Oh, no, I didn't."

Violet kidded her sister, "Nell's anger over the scene probably put off more colors than those kids did."

Nell tilted her head to the side. "Are those kids actors or did someone actually film an episode of real bullying?"

"They're actors," Rob told her. "Maybe that's why you didn't see any colors. Maybe the kids aren't really feeling the emotions they're presenting. Let's try another one."

The lights went off and the next scenario began to play on the screen. A young woman in her early twenties walked along a city street in the dark. It must have been late because the sidewalks were deserted. Suddenly, a man entered the scene and followed the woman down the street. When he caught up to her, he grabbed her long hair from behind and pulled her towards him. The woman struck out at the man. He wrapped his hands around her throat and squeezed.

The video scenario ended and Rob turned the lights on.

Nell's facial muscles were tense and her breathing was faster than when the video began. She could feel little beads of perspiration roll down her back.

"Anything?" Rob asked.

Nell's hands were clasped in her lap. "Yes. Colors. Maybe I saw the colors because the actors are drawing on their own emotions to play the parts. I saw bright red and a deep, dark red coming off the man. The woman sent out waves of orange and black, and there was an aura all around her pulsing with purple and green."

"What do those colors mean?" Rob asked.

Nell let out a long breath of air. "When this color thing first started, I had the idea that each color was representative of just a few things. I'm learning that shades of the same color seem to have different meanings so the reds coming off the man probably stand for anger and death. These particular purple and green hues that the woman gave off indicate fear and sadness. The black symbolizes fear and hopelessness and the light shade of orange might mean a missed warning."

Violet and Rob had their eyes focused on Nell.

"That's incredible." Rob kept staring at his friend.

Sitting up with pride, Violet smiled. "Well, she's my sister, so of course she's incredible."

Nell stood and went to the side table for a glass of water. "I don't like doing this. It's hard. The scenes are very disturbing. My head is starting to hurt."

"We can quit for the day," Rob said. "We've determined that you're able to see emotions revealed as colors even from a film or a video. It doesn't only work in person. This is big. We can do some experimenting. It's very exciting."

Nell gave him a look. "Don't turn me into some lab rat."

Violet turned back to the blank screen. "Was that situation we just watched of the man attacking the woman from a self-defense course?"

"Yes, it is." Ron typed on his laptop, but glanced over at Nell. "Did you sign up to take the self-defense class the university is putting on?"

"We did. Violet and I are both going to take it."

"Excellent." Rob went back to typing.

"If we keep watching that scene, will they show us what to do in case someone comes up behind us and starts choking us?"

Rob said, "Yeah, they do."

"Can we watch it?" Violet asked. "Is it okay with you, Nell?"

"Sure, as long as it's short."

Rob went over to the projector and pressed play. A woman came on the screen and spoke about what to do in the situation. The man again approached the young woman walking on the sidewalk, but this time when he yanked on her hair, she spun around and squatted, pulling the guy off balance. She elbowed him in the gut and ran.

Violet applauded.

The speaker came back on the screen and spoke about what do if someone attempted to strangle you. The young woman is shown with the man squeezing her throat. She placed one hand on one side of the man's face, and the other hand on the other side. Then she used her thumbs to press into the man's eyes. The man let her go and she ran.

"I would never have thought to do that." Violet got up and practiced on Rob.

"Don't press on my eyes," he protested. "Just hold the position."

Nell couldn't help but chuckle at what was going on.

"Come and try it." Violet encouraged her sister.

Nell walked over to where they were practicing

an attack. She stood in front of Rob and he placed his hands gently around her neck, and she felt warmth spread through her veins.

"Now put your hands up in between his arms," Violet told her. "Put your hands on the sides of his face, then press your thumbs into his eyes. Gently, of course."

When Nell put her hands on Rob's face, Violet swore his cheeks flared pink, and she didn't need Nell's interpretation of colors to know why he was blushing.

The researcher and the lab rat stood there for a few moments, smiling, and staring into each other's eyes.

"HE WAS BLUSHING," Violet said.

"No, he wasn't. He gets red in the face when he's excited about his work."

"I saw the light in his eyes when he was looking at you."

With a laugh, Nell shook her head. "You're imagining things."

"I think Rob is falling for you."

"We've known each other for years," Nell

protested. "Some blossom of interest isn't going to suddenly burst forth from the ground. If Rob blushed, it's because we felt silly standing there with him trying to choke me, and me attempting to gouge his eyes out."

Going up the steps to the police station, Violet said, "We'll table this discussion for now."

The sisters were met in the lobby by Chief Lambert and the three went into his office.

"I'm glad you came by," the chief said. "Are you both okay?

Nell and Violet looked confused by his question.

"When I texted, you mentioned you were at the hospital."

"Oh, I see." Nell explained that her ophthalmologist worked at the university hospital and they were there for some testing.

Chief Lambert's expression was one of relief. "That's good to hear. I was worried something was wrong with one of you."

After they took seats around a small table, Nell spoke. "We've been thinking a lot about Adam Timson and the case. A neighbor of ours was speculating about Adam and he told us about an article he'd read a few years ago. It was about the federal witness protection program."

The chief's eyebrows went up.

Violet said, "We're thinking there's a possibility that Adam Timson might be in the witness protection program."

The chief gave a nod. "As it turns out, we've been wondering the very same thing."

14

"We need to tell John and Ida that his idea about Adam being in witness protection was probably right." Nell stood at the kitchen counter preparing a salad for dinner.

Violet checked the tacos warming in the oven. "Chief Lambert should bring John on as a consultant to the police."

Iris and Oscar sat in the kitchen watching the young women make dinner hoping some food item might drop on the floor and they could help clean up by eating it.

"How long do you think it will take the state marshals' office to get back to the chief?" Nell wondered aloud.

"Who knows? Soon, I hope. If they confirm Adam is in the program, it would explain a lot of what's been going on."

When Nell and Violet were in Chief Lambert's office, he told them that law enforcement shared their suspicions that Adam might be in witness protection and that he'd made a call to the marshals' state office to inquiry about the possibility. He had yet to hear back from them.

"Will they tell the chief one way or the other?" Nell asked. "The information must be highly confidential and they're probably very careful about revealing anyone's identity ... even to a police chief. There are some crooked members of law enforcement out there. Who knows if a police officer is connected to some criminals? I'd bet the marshals are extremely wary about sharing any information about who is in the program."

"Those are good points." Violet removed the baking sheet of tacos from the oven.

The dogs wagged their tails and sniffed the air.

"Don't worry," Violet told Iris and Oscar. "We saved some plain chicken for both of you."

It was dark when the sisters carried the food to the deck and after giving each dog a plate of chicken, they lit the candles on the table and sat down to eat.

It was a warm, clear night with a light, pleasant breeze coming in off the ocean.

"It's pretty clear Adam is in danger whether he's in the witness protection program or not." Nell took two tacos from the serving dish. "The gunman at his house is proof of that. Where did Adam go? Is our goal now to find Adam and whoever is after him?"

"How can you help them find Adam?" Violet sipped from her glass of seltzer. "The man didn't leave much of a trace. The chief said they're going to search his car for any clues. After Adam left the car behind the fast food restaurant and threw Oscar's things in the dumpster, he must have walked across the street to the bus station. He's long gone by now, and who knows to where? Did the police ask the employees at the bus station if they recognized Adam?"

"They did ask. No one remembers Adam being there. The police showed them a copy of Adam's license photo and a mock-up of Adam with darker hair and glasses. No luck. And the security camera at the bus station wasn't working."

Violet groaned. "Bad luck all around."

"Maybe it's good luck for Adam if he doesn't want to be found."

"He can't run forever," Violet said. "He'll need a

job and a place to live, and he'll need new identification with a new name in order to keep safe. He'll need a new social security number, too, in order to be able to work. The cash he took out of the bank won't last forever, then what will he do? If he uses the name Adam Timson, whoever is after him will find him eventually. He's in a real mess."

"If he's in witness protection, why didn't he call the marshals for help?" Nell asked.

Violet shrugged. "Maybe he didn't trust them for some reason?"

Nell's face fell. "If Adam feels he can't trust them, he's really in trouble."

"Is his phone still functioning?"

"No," Nell said. "The chief told me it must have been destroyed right before Adam fled. There's no signal. It can't be traced."

"So if a U.S. marshal tried to contact Adam, he wouldn't be able to reach him," Violet noted. "Maybe Adam is going to show up at one of the marshals' offices in person to ask for help. Maybe he's traveling to someplace he feels safe, to an office where he knows a marshal he trusts."

Nell was about to bite into a taco when she paused. "That's an interesting theory. Wouldn't it be great to know Adam's background? Wherever he used to live, is probably the place where he knows a marshal."

"Is there a chance we could figure out where he came from?" Violet's voice sounded excited. "Want to do some internet sleuthing?"

The sisters finished the meal, cleaned up, and sat together on the living room sofa with Violet resting her laptop in her knees.

"Where do we start?" Nell asked.

"Let's search Adam's name." Violet tapped on the keyboard and only a few things came up ... his website, the name of his company and its contact information. Every other entry was for a different Adam Timson.

"Would someone in witness protection keep his name? His first name?" Nell asked.

Violet looked up the U.S. witness protection program and read from one of the entries. "The program is also called the Witness Security Program. It's under the direction of the Department of Justice, but it's run by the U.S. Marshals Service. Witnesses often keep their own first names or take on a name that is very similar. Their last names often start with the same letter as their old last names."

"Why?" Nell asked.

"It says that way the witness can catch themselves before making a mistake and writing their old last names." Violet kept reading. "Here's something interesting. Witnesses are supposed to lie all the time and never, ever reveal their past identities to anyone, not even a new spouse."

"Wow." Nell's eyes widened. "That must be very difficult to do."

Violet read from the article. "If the marriage ever goes bad and the witness revealed his or her past information to the spouse, the spouse could use it out of spite to get the person into serious trouble."

"Does the article say if the witness can stay close to where they're originally from?" Nell asked.

"I don't see anything about that." Violet scanned a different search entry. "This one reports that no witness in the program has ever been killed, but if the witness leaves the program, they're in very real danger. It tells about people who have contacted old friends or returned to their former city, and they ended up getting killed. This article states the importance of never returning, even for a short time, to your old life."

"It seems like very good advice." Nell wrapped her arms around herself. "Imagine having to leave everything you've known and never being able to go back? It's so sad."

"This article says there's a safe house outside of Washington, D.C. where new witnesses are taken for orientation. The place is even able to withstand a bombing," Violet said.

"Do you think Adam would try to get to that safe house?" Nell asked.

"I have no idea. How do we have any chance of finding information on Adam? There's nothing to go on. I don't even know what to enter to search on," Violet said.

"Try a search on U.S. Marshals in the D.C. area and see what comes up?" Nell suggested.

Violet tapped at the keys. "There are lists of district offices and courthouses. There's a list of fugitives from the area. There's an entry on how to become a marshal. Not much help."

Looking at the laptop screen, something caught Nell's eye and she gestured to an article. "How about that one? What's that about?"

Violet clicked on it and began to read. "Oh."

"Oh, what? What does it say?" Nell tried to read over her sister's shoulder.

"It's a report on a man who worked as a clerk in the U.S. Marshal's office in D.C. He lived in Arlington. He's dead."

"What happened to him?"

Violet made eye contact with Nell. "He was killed."

Nell's mouth dropped open.

"An intruder broke into his house and shot the man. It says the motive was theft."

"When did this happen?" Nell squinted to try and see the words on the screen.

A little gasp escaped from Violet's throat. "Four days before Adam took off."

The sisters stared at one another.

"Does this have something to do with Adam's disappearance?" Nell's voice shook. "I'm going to text Chief Lambert."

Shortly after the text was sent, the chief called Nell's phone.

"I just finished speaking with a marshal out of the Massachusetts office. He wouldn't say if Adam is in the program. He took my information and told me he would pass it on. I might receive a call on the matter. Might, was the emphasized word. I don't know if they'll admit to me if Adam is in the program, but I'm expecting a call from them to find out everything we know."

"I guess that's expected," Nell said. "They won't take a chance with a witness's safety."

"What you sent me is very interesting," the chief

said. "We'll look into it. We've requested records for Adam's phone. We couldn't do it earlier because there wasn't cause, but after the gunman was in Adam's house and shot the neighbor, we were able to legally make the request to obtain the phone records. When we receive them, we'll look to see if there was any contact between Adam and this murdered marshal. I'll let you know what we find out as soon as we have the records. Good work, you two. Let me know if anything else comes up."

Nell clicked off and looked at her sister. "I have a strong feeling that Adam and that clerk at the marshal's office have a connection. Maybe Adam called him and couldn't reach him. Maybe Adam found out what happened or became frightened when he couldn't communicate with his contact. This might be the reason Adam took off."

15

D rinking her morning coffee, Nell sat outside on the deck reading the news on her laptop. She had news alerts on her computer related to her topics of interest having to do with art, the town, New England happenings, the weather, business, and tetrachromats.

Nell clicked on a news article about an amateur photography exhibit in Providence, Rhode Island and read about the entries and prizes. Some of the best photographs in the exhibit were reproduced in the article and when she scrolled to look at them, she almost fell out of her chair.

A man stood on a wind-swept beach in front of a stormy sea facing the camera, but looking off past the photographer to something far in the distance. A dog sat off to the side.

Adam Timson. The caption said, "*Adam T., Blue-water Cove beach.*"

With a racing heart, Nell looked for the name of the photographer. *Bonnie Plant.*

Bonnie was the bank teller who had come outside to speak to Nell and Peter about Adam.

"Violet." Nell called to her sister. "Come out here. You have to see this."

Violet appeared at the screen door in her pajama shorts and tank top. "What's up?"

"Look at this." Nell turned her laptop so her sister could see the picture.

Violet came out carrying her bagel with cream cheese, and when she bent to get a look at the article on Nell's laptop, she almost choked on her bite of bagel. "What the heck is this? Adam is in a photograph in an exhibit? How? He wouldn't allow that."

"The teller from the bank, Bonnie Plant, took the photo and submitted it to the contest. You can't miss that it's Adam. Someone who has it in for Adam must have seen the exhibit, or someone who knows the person who wants Adam dead must have seen the exhibit. It's been open for three weeks. The title of the photograph includes where it was taken ...

Bluewater Cove beach." Nell stood up and paced around the deck. "It wouldn't be hard to find Adam with that information. Gosh. Bonnie Plant couldn't have known what she was doing when she submitted the photo."

"Or could she?" Violet asked with narrowed eyes.

"We need to go talk to Bonnie. I'll text Elizabeth and ask her if she can open the store this morning. Let's go to the bank when it opens." Nell hurried to her laptop. "I'll send the link to this article to Chief Lambert."

Nell and Violet waited in the bank parking lot and when they saw Bonnie Plant pull in and get out of her car, the sisters hurried to catch up to her.

Nell called the woman's name and Bonnie turned around. "Oh, hi, it's you. It's Nell, right?"

Nell introduced Violet. "Do you have a few minutes to talk? It's about Adam."

Bonnie's face dropped and her hand covered her heart. "Is he okay?"

"Is there somewhere we can talk?" Nell asked.

"The bank doesn't open for forty-five minutes. We can use one of the offices." Bonnie led them into the bank and into an office. "We can talk in here. This is the assistant manager's office. She's out this week."

The three women pulled up chairs into a semi-circle.

"Have the police found Adam?" Bonnie's eyes were full of worry.

"No, they haven't." Nell thought she should be careful how she worded her sentences so Bonnie wouldn't become defensive. "Could you tell us more about your relationship with Adam?"

Blinking, Bonnie sat straighter in her seat. "I ... I didn't have a *relationship* with him."

"Were you friends?"

"Not exactly."

Nell could feel anger rising in her chest at Bonnie's reluctance to be forthcoming, but she pushed it down so Bonnie wouldn't notice. "You talked to Adam at the pub one night, and you went to Bluewater beach with him. I saw the photograph you did of him at the beach. You're very talented."

Bonnie's features softened slightly. "Thank you. Yes, I was at the pub and talked to Adam. We went to the beach one day."

"Did you get together more than that? Had you been doing things together?" Violet questioned.

Bonnie blew out a long breath. "Look, I liked Adam. He's such a nice guy. I ran into him at the pub one night, like I told you. We talked for a while. I asked him if he'd like to go for a hike in the state park one day, and to my surprise he agreed. We went for a hike one Saturday morning. We were out for hours, hiking around the meadows, and the lakes, and up to the top of the hill. There's such a beautiful view from there. We brought our lunch and ate on the boulders in the sun. It was a perfect day."

"Were you together as friends?" Violet asked.

"I was attracted to Adam, but I didn't want to scare him off. We did a few things together as friends." Bonnie sighed. "He's not an easy person to get to know. He's cautious. He's great to talk with, but if the subject turns to him, he clams up. I figured it was his way of taking things slow, of not sharing much about himself until he was sure he liked me or trusted me or whatever was in his head. I was fine with it. I respected it."

"Adam posed for the picture you took of him?" Nell couldn't believe he would do that.

"No, he didn't know I took it. His attention was far away. I thought it came out great. I knew there was a photo exhibition and contest coming up in

Providence and I decided to enter. I didn't think Adam would mind. I hoped he'd be flattered."

"Was he?" Nell asked, believing she probably knew the answer … Adam would not be pleased.

Bonnie said, "I made a copy for him. When I gave it to him, he looked horrified. I was taken aback by his reaction. When I told him I'd sent it to a contest and exhibition, he asked if I could withdraw it. I was shocked. He told me he was a private person and didn't want to have his photo on display. I told him I was sorry … I should have asked his permission first. I called the organizers, but they told me I'd won a prize and that it stated in the rules that a winning photograph had to remain in the exhibit until it was over. I was so distressed that Adam was upset about it." The young woman wrung her hands together in her lap. "I figured I'd blown it with Adam."

"How many times did you get together with Adam?" Violet asked.

"Not many. Maybe five or six. We went hiking a couple of times. We went to the beach on a stormy day to walk around. I invited him over to have appetizers and to watch a baseball game. We went to a movie once. I think that was about it. It was always as friends, nothing more than that."

"Did Adam seem like he might be interested in a relationship?" Nell asked.

"Really? I don't know if we were headed in that direction or not. He never tried to kiss me or hold my hand. It was clearly a friend type of thing."

"Did you learn anything about Adam's background when you were getting together?" Violet asked. "Did he tell you anything about his past? His growing up years?"

"I asked him where he grew up. He told me in the Midwest, but before I could ask him where, he turned the conversation to me. He did that frequently. If I asked about his background or his family or where he went to school, he maneuvered the discussion to me or to a different topic. I didn't even realize it at the time. I thought about it later and became aware that Adam never really answered any of my questions about his life before he moved to Saxonwood. It felt a little weird to me. I worried maybe he was a criminal or something, but I brushed that away. Adam is too nice to be a criminal."

"When did you tell him his photo was in the exhibit?" Nell asked.

"A few days before he took off." Bonnie bit her lower lip. "Do you think that's why he left? Do you think he thought I was too forward? Is that why he left? Maybe he thought I was trying to get too close to him? Maybe he didn't want to reject me outright and hurt my feelings. Maybe he just decided to leave town and avoid the whole thing."

"We've never met Adam," Violet pointed out. "We really don't know him."

Bonnie gave a sad nod of her head.

"Did Adam mention anything about himself?" Nell asked the woman hoping she knew some little thing.

Adam told me a little about his business, what he does for his clients. He builds websites and does graphic design work. He told me he used to live in central Massachusetts for a while. Um, let's see. His parents are dead. He enjoys watching sports, baseball is his favorite. He likes to hike and camp. He told me he'd been all through the state park. Oh, he said he'd like to have a sports car someday, but he can't afford one." Bonnie's forehead scrunched up in thought. "I think that's all."

"That's a lot. Thanks for telling us what you know." Nell smiled at the woman.

"Do you think Adam took off for a while because he needed some space?" Bonnie asked. "Do you think he'll come back?"

"We don't really know if Adam's gone on a trip or if he's decided to move to a different place," Violet said.

Bonnie said, "I wonder if Adam knows there was an intruder in his house? I bet he doesn't know. He told me he had good neighbors, he liked them. I think he'd be horrified to know someone broke into his house and shot his neighbor. If he knew, I bet he'd come right back."

Nell disagreed with Bonnie. She was pretty sure if Adam knew his neighbor had been shot by a gunman from inside his house, he'd never, ever set foot in the area again.

16

_____

The sisters took the dogs for a walk in the state park just after the sun came up to avoid the heat and to get a walk in before they opened the store for the day. Iris and Oscar happily trotted along the path sniffing here and there, playing with a stick they found and stopping to watch a heron on the other side of a pond.

The dappled light sparkled with thousands of colors complementing the shades and hues in the trees, leaves, grasses, and wildflowers. The early morning air promised a hot and humid day.

"Let's go to the beach for a swim after work today," Violet suggested. "We haven't been swimming as much as usual this summer."

"Our spare time has been getting used up with

other things," Nell said. "Maybe law enforcement will find Adam soon and place him again in a safe location. It must be incredibly hard to start all over again somewhere new."

"But," Violet said, "it's better than being dead. I wonder what Adam testified in court about ... what kind of a crime was it? Who did he testify against?"

"It must have been something serious. As soon as the criminals found out where he was, they moved pretty fast. It must be related to gang or mob activity."

"I don't know if I have the guts to do such a thing." Violet almost shuddered. "Testifying, being relocated, being afraid my cover would be blown and the killers would be after me. I could never rest or feel safe or comfortable again." She eyed her sister. "You'd have to come with me."

"Hmm. I'd have to think about that," Nell kidded. "Do me a favor and don't witness anything dangerous."

"I'll do my best."

After forty minutes of walking, they reached the spot on the trail that Oscar had been so interested in the last time they were in the state park, and the dog trotted right into the woods and began sniffing and whining.

"Is this where Oscar was fussing about something the last time we were here?" Violet asked.

"It is. He remembers something interesting was in there." Nell walked to the edge of the trail, pushed some branches to the side and joined the dog behind the trees. "I don't see any tracks, but it's been so dry lately nothing would show up in the dirt." She looked up in the tree branches, and turned in a circle checking for any signs that a deer or a bear or a coyote had been lurking.

Since they had been on the trail at a later time of day the last time, the sun was at a different angle and was shining down on the forest floor from a lower position in the sky so Nell expected to see a change in the colors she saw.

Nell stiffened. There were sparkles of yellow and white mixed in with the other shades she saw ... the exact same hues of yellow she noticed the other day. The sparkles seemed like remnants of what she'd seen previously. She took her time staring at the colors, and every time she saw the particular shade of yellow with shimmers of white hovering near, a prickly feeling picked at her skin.

"What are you doing in there?" Violet asked peeking through the branches at her sister and Oscar.

Oscar had his nose to the ground and was rushing around under the brush and through the undergrowth like a bloodhound.

"There's something funny about the light." Nell kicked gently at the ground with the toe of her hiking boot.

"Funny like haha or funny like unusual?"

"Unusual."

Violet frowned. "Great. What's so unusual ... besides you being able to see things other people can't?"

"Some of the colors seem to have been here from the last time we were here." Nell moved slowly around looking for the yellow-white shades.

"What does that mean?"

"I saw a particular shade of yellow along with white when we were here before. I can see what seems to be the residue of those colors." Nell moved branches to see the spots.

"You mean that some of the colors you saw last time are still here? Like the same colors lingered? Color is just light. Why do you think those colors you saw last time are the same ones you see now? Colors aren't something tangible, you can't leave them behind to find another day like you dropped some pennies on the ground and they're still there. I don't get what you mean."

Nell came out of the woods. "I don't get it either, but some of the colors look older, not like the yellows and whites that are here today. It feels like a little of them got left behind and stayed here."

"This is too weird for me." Violet groaned. "What does the yellow mean?"

"It feels like ... happiness." Nell looked directly at her sister. "The white that I see feels like purity, like something ... sacred."

Violet blew out a long sigh. "I don't even know what to say."

"I don't understand it. I'm just explaining what I see and how it makes me feel."

"Well, Oscar must feel it too because he's still sniffing around back there."

"I need to talk to Rob," Nell said softly.

NELL AND ROB sat across from each other at the table in his office. He'd been listening intently to what Nell had been telling him about what she saw in the woods early that morning.

"Is it possible to see *older* colors ... colors I saw from a few days ago?"

Rob breathed deeply. "You don't think the colors you saw in the woods were the result of today's light?"

"No. The particles of yellow and white I saw today looked older somehow."

Rob's eyes narrowed as he thought about what Nell was telling him. "So to put it simply, visible light is a form of electromagnetic radiation. Visible light can be explained as wavelengths that can be seen by the human eye. Colors are properties of light and the cone cells in the eye. The cones are receivers that are tuned to the wavelengths of the narrow band of visible light. Things don't have color, per se, they give off light that shows as color to the eye."

Nell nodded. She'd heard this many times before.

"Now, as far as seeing *older* colors ... an atom that has mass will break into smaller particles and will eventually die. Photons are carriers of light. Do photons have mass? Because if they do, they will eventually break down and die. Photons are said to have zero mass. But things can get sticky here. For a variety of reasons that we won't go into, let's say that maybe a photon does have mass. Then the question is ... how long can the photon live? From a human being's perspective, light can live for about a billion years. There's a whole bunch of other stuff that goes into this discussion, but it's possible that a visible wavelength photon could be stable for a billion years."

Nell's face brightened and her voice was full of excitement. "So I *can* see older light which means I can see older colors?"

"If anyone but you asked that question, I'd say no. But since it's *you* asking me if it's possible for you to see older light and colors, I'd say I wouldn't bet against it."

A wide smile spread over Nell's face. "Something was in the woods a few days ago that left behind some traces. Maybe it was an animal that didn't notice the dogs and was in a state of peace and contentment and that's what was left on the ground in the woods. It must have seen the dogs when Oscar whined, and it left very fast. Maybe it left in such a hurry, it left behind traces of how it was feeling. Maybe I can see animals' emotions and feelings, too."

Rob smiled at his friend. "That would be pretty cool."

"The really cool part," Nell said, "is that I could still sense the colors left behind days later."

"We'll have to test this hypothesis." Rob scribbled in a notebook.

Nell's smile faded. "I wonder if I can pick up on the emotions that human's leave behind. That could be very useful in a criminal investigation."

Rob looked up from making his notes. "It could be very upsetting as well. If it was a murder, you wouldn't want to be able to feel what a victim experienced."

Nell's expression turned to one of panic. "That would be frightening."

"You've never seen what you're calling *old* colors before?"

"No. I never noticed until this morning. Something was different about the way they looked. Sort of lightly faded. Kind of like the warm patina an old wooden table gets after years and years of use. The yellow and white I saw this morning looked slightly different and they made me think they were older colors."

"You never cease to amaze me." Rob shook his head.

"I'm always trying to come up with some strange,

new thing that will stun and astound the intelligent research scientist and doctor," Nell teased.

"You've been doing a good job lately. Keep up the good work."

Nell's face took on a serious expression. "Why did this happen to me? That I can see people's emotions as colors? Was it the tornado that did it?"

Rob looked up from the notes he was writing. "I think so. There are some physiological things that can be traced to or are thought to derive from emotional upheaval. Your experience in that storm shook you to your very core. The shock to your system as you looked sudden death in the face was powerful and violent. You're still feeling the after effects."

Nell nodded. "My overpowering fear of storms nearly strangles me whenever I hear the wind kick up. It's faded a little ... a very, very little bit." The young woman's eyes widened. "My terror from wind and weather will hopefully fade into the distance someday. Will my new ability to see colors from people fade away eventually?"

Rob looked deep into Nell's eyes. "That's a very good question."

17

The restaurant-pub was crowded with customers enjoying their meals and drinks and the live band playing in the corner near the bar. The atmosphere was upbeat and fun and Nell, Violet, Dani, and Peter were having a good time while they waited for the meals to arrive.

Peter said, "I hate to bring up the case, but Chief Lambert asked me to pass some information on to you."

Nell and Violet lost their cheerful expressions.

"The phone records show that Adam Timson called and texted that U.S Marshal who was found murdered in Arlington, Virginia many times in the days leading up to his taking off."

Nell's shoulders slumped. "That guy must have been Adam's contact in the witness protection program."

"The killer must have thought if he took out the marshal, then there wouldn't be anyone to warn Adam that his identity had become compromised," Peter told them. "At least, not right away. Maybe they thought killing the marshal would buy them time to get to Adam."

"So Chief Lambert thinks Adam is in the protection program?" Nell asked.

"That's what he's thinking. He still hasn't heard anything from the marshals' office in Boston which probably means Adam is in their database. They're not going to confirm anything in case doing so puts Adam at risk."

"How did anyone know it was Adam in that photo from the photography exhibition in Providence?" Dani asked as she lifted an appetizer from the plate of mini pizzas in the center of the table. "How did the criminals find out so fast?"

Peter took a swallow of his beer. "Who knows what Adam testified about that was so dangerous he went into the protection program? There are connections and links throughout the criminal world. Someone must have been at the exhibition, recognized Adam, and passed the word on to the interested party. It was an unexpected, but fortunate bit of luck for the criminals. It happens."

"When Bonnie Plant showed Adam the photo she'd taken of him and told him it was being displayed in a big exhibition in Providence, he must have freaked out." Violet wiped her fingers on her napkin.

"And when he tried to get in touch with the marshal assigned to him and the man wouldn't reply, well, that must have set off alarm bells and he knew he had to set his escape plans in motion," Nell surmised.

When Dani shook her head, her blond hair moved over her shoulders. "People in witness protection have some kind of escape plan ready to go?"

"I don't know if they have a plan in place," Peter said, "I would think they needed to talk to their marshal for advice and instructions. The person would need a whole new identity created and the paperwork to go with it. My guess is that Adam is winging it until he feels he can safely contact another marshal. I bet he's lying low somewhere trying to figure out what to do."

Nell said, "I bet he doesn't know who to trust.

He's probably afraid to trust anyone, law enforcement included. There are bad guys everywhere. He can't take the chance."

"You don't think that teller, Bonnie whatever, has anything to do with the criminals, do you?" Dani asked.

"I don't." Peter ordered another drink from the waiter. "Bonnie Plant has been working and living in Saxonwood for years."

Dani looked skeptical. "That doesn't mean she's innocent of wrongdoing. She might have some connection with the criminal world, a brother, a friend, and one thing led to another. Maybe someone saw Bonnie's photo of Adam at her house and the word spread from one gangster to another. It doesn't matter if she's lived in the area for years, Bonnie could have connections with criminals and she could have had a hand in this mess."

Violet said, "She also might have been offended and angry that Adam didn't seem to have a romantic interest in her so if she had a chance to hurt him, maybe she took it. You should talk to her again," she told Peter. "Or look more closely into her background and her contacts."

Something about the discussion tugged at Nell, but she couldn't figure out why.

"Where do you think Adam ran to?" Dani asked. "Any ideas?"

Peter shook his head. "Really? No. Adam lived in central Massachusetts for a number of years before he moved to Saxonwood, but prior to that, he's practically a ghost. There's very little trail back to his past and the things that *are* there were probably created by the protection program. A person has to have some kind of a trail back to his early life, no matter how thin it is, otherwise it's fishy and raises questions and suspicions. So, no, we don't have any idea where Adam might have taken off to. He could be anywhere a bus or a train travels."

The meals arrived and everyone began to eat.

"I can't help thinking there has to be a clue somewhere in his house," Violet said. "Some little thing that could help the police find him. His car was searched, right?"

Peter took a bite of his eggplant parmesan. "It was. They went over it carefully. Nothing was found."

"Maybe you should look at the house again," Violet suggested. "It couldn't hurt to take another look."

"An officer drives by almost every day to be sure nothing is amiss with the place," Peter said.

"How is the neighbor, Scott Mckenzie?" Nell asked. "Is he doing okay?"

"The chief told us the neighbor will be going home in a day or two. He's lucky to be alive. Just a few millimeters in either direction, and that bullet would have killed him."

Dani groaned. "If I were Scott McKenzie, I think I'd move away. I don't think I could live next door to the place where I was nearly killed."

"He's lived on that street for a long time," Violet said. "I'll bet he and his wife will stay there."

After dinner, Nell and Violet walked along the brick sidewalks past the shops and restaurants near the harbor heading towards home.

"I was thinking," Nell said. "We know Adam lived in Worcester for six years and we know he's owned his house for about a year and a half. Before he bought his house, he lived in an apartment in Saxon-wood for a year. That's a total of eight and half years. If Worcester was his first home after entering the protection program, then the court case he testified during, might have been eight or nine years ago. We could do some internet investigating to see if we could find some big case that was happening at the time."

"The police must have done that already," Violet

said. "And Worcester might not have been Adam's first place to hide. I don't think we have enough information to make an internet search work. If it was that easy to find someone in witness protection, it wouldn't be a very good program."

"I guess you're right," Nell said reluctantly. "So many dead ends. Maybe Adam will contact a marshals' office soon and we can stop worrying about him."

The sisters arrived home, changed into pajamas, and made tea. They sat with the dogs in the living room and decided to watch a movie before going to bed.

Iris stretched out on the area rug and Oscar sat at the sliding doors peering out at the dark night. Something caught his eye outside and he tapped his tail against the wood floor.

"Is somebody walking down the street?" Nell asked the dog.

Oscar turned his head to her and his wagging became more vigorous.

Nell patted her knee and called the dog to her side, and when he trotted over to her and put his head on her leg, she ran her hand over his soft fur. "Such a good dog."

The dog's coat began to shimmer with tiny

colored sparkles, a mix of yellows and white that glimmered off and on like the light of a firefly.

"Are you happy, good boy?" Nell asked with a smile. "Are you happy here with us?"

Oscar's tail bumped against the floor and the dog wiggled a bit, his eyes shining brightly.

"I see colors on Oscar," Nell told her sister.

With her eyes half-open, Violet yawned and turned her head to look. "What colors do you see? Nothing bad, I hope."

"Yellows and white. They're flashing all over his body."

"Yellow means happy and white means purity. Our canine companion is feeling good. The colors are the same as the ones you saw when we were on the trail in the state park," Violet noted.

Nell looked from Oscar to Violet. "Oh. Is that why I saw the yellow and white particles shimmering in the thicket the other day? Were the colors left there by Oscar the morning he was so fascinated with whatever was hiding in the trees?"

"Could be, now that you're able to see animal emotions," Violet told her, "and you can see emotions that were left behind in a place and not just sensations being felt in the present. Your abilities are really expanding."

"Oscar is content here," Nell said. "He's comfortable now. When he first came home with us, he occasionally showed some signs of stress ... panting, shaking, nervousness, but he's calmed down and settled in. He and Iris get along so well. He seems happy to be with the three of us."

"He's a wonderful dog. I'm perfectly happy to keep him forever." Violet shifted her position on the sofa and rested her head on a small decorative pillow.

"You hear that, Oscar? You can stay with us as long as you like. You have a home here if you want it." Nell scratched behind the dog's ears.

Oscar put his front paws on the sofa and leaned close to Nell to run his pink tongue over her cheek.

"You're the best boy dog there is," Nell told him.

When Iris lifted her head and glanced over, Nell said, "And you're the best girl dog there is."

Satisfied, Iris placed her head back down on the rug.

Nell leaned against the sofa and contentedly watched the yellow and white flashes flicker on and off in Oscar's soft fur.

18

———

"I've been waiting for you." Wearing shorts and a T-shirt, Rob hurried to Nell when he saw her approaching from across the campus green.

Nell checked her watch. "I'm early. Why are you in such a rush today?"

"I want to take you to the other side of the student center." Rob spoke quickly and he walked briskly away from the bench he'd been sitting on.

"Why? Aren't we going running?" Nell hurried to catch up to him.

"Yes, but first, I want you to see something." Rob opened the glass door to the student center and held it open for Nell.

Summer classes were in session and students

worked at tables or in leather chairs set up in small groups scattered around the space. Inside was a coffee and dessert café, a sandwich and soup shop, and several other food places to choose from. Floor to ceiling glass windows allowed in plenty of light to create an airy, bright space to meet friends or to quietly work and study.

"Where are we going?" Nell was becoming impatient.

Rob stopped outside the campus book store. "Right here." He took Nell's arm and maneuvered her near the wall. "Let's do an impromptu experiment. Something happened here a few minutes ago. Look around."

Nell shifted uncomfortably from foot to foot. "For what?"

Rob lowered his voice. "Do you see any colors?"

"I *always* see colors." Nell answered with a snippy tone. She didn't really like the student center, it was full of competing shades of colors that sometimes made her head hurt or her stomach feel ill. She was also feeling slightly annoyed by the demands of an unexpected test, but she took a deep breath and glanced around the spot Rob had taken her to knowing that he wanted to find out if she could pick up on some emotions left behind by someone who had been there.

Nell looked for colors that seemed older searching for hues that appeared a little less vibrant or a bit faded.

And then she noticed them. Tiny glimmering particles floating in the air like fairy dust ... green, white, yellow ... twirling together and sparkling on and off. Nell's heart filled with joy and happiness and a smile spread over her face.

She told Rob what she saw. "The green color is soft and light, not the green of envy or jealousy. The yellow makes me feel happy. The white is pure and perfect." She turned to the researcher. "Something good happened here. Someone was full of joy. Maybe more than one person."

Rob's face brightened with a wide smile. "I walked past here about thirty minutes ago. I stopped to read a message on my phone. When I looked up, I saw two medical interns sitting on the bench in the corner. I've met them. They're married. The man hugged and kissed his wife and then he jumped up and yelled, 'we're going to have a baby.'"

Nell nodded. "Green can symbolize new life."

Rob touched her arm and said excitedly, "You saw

it. You could see that something happy took place here, something important that caused strong emotions. The couple's interaction happened more than a half hour ago, but the colors still lingered and you can see them. It's remarkable. It is truly astounding."

Nell's heart swelled at Rob's elation, but then worry clouded her mind. "You haven't told anyone about this, have you?"

Rob's face lost its smile. "No. No one."

"It concerns me. I don't want to become a freak ... tested, stared at, discussed like I'm not in the room. I'll end up in a circus sideshow of researchers, scientists, news reporters." The huge space with its millions of colors started to close in on Nell. "I need some fresh air." She bolted for the doors with Rob hurrying after her.

Jogging to the far side of the campus green, Nell took a seat on a shaded bench tucked under a few tall Maple trees. She closed her eyes and breathed deeply and slowly.

Rob sat down next to her, but he didn't speak, knowing from years of friendship that Nell needed a few minutes to allow her eyes to rest and to calm her mind.

"I'm okay." Nell opened her eyes and accepted a water bottle from Rob.

"I understand. We don't have to do any more tests or experiments. We don't have to share your unique ability with anyone. Whatever you want to do is fine with me."

"I need to think about it." Nell sipped the water. "Could I be anonymous if you published an article?"

"Yes. I wouldn't name you in an article. But the time might come when other researchers would need to repeat the tests to corroborate my findings. You could refuse, of course."

Nell nodded. "Okay. Let's take it slow. Continue with the tests and experiments and gather some information. Then we can go from there."

"Sounds good. Slow and steady." Rob gave her an encouraging smile. "You'll decide if we proceed or if we stop."

Tension drained from Nell's muscles and her sense of panic faded away. "You're a good friend to me."

They sat together under the trees for a few more minutes admiring the beautiful campus and enjoying the shady spot.

"Want to go for our run now?" Nell asked.

"You feel up to it?"

"Yeah." Nell nodded. "It will do me good to be out on the trails in the woods."

"Okay, let's go." Rob stood up and offered his hand to pull the young woman from her spot on the bench.

With a smile, Nell took his hand and rose to her feet, and then the two of them jogged across the campus, down the pretty streets of Bluewater Cove to the harbor, and then up the road that would take them to the state park.

DAY HAD TURNED into night as Nell sat in the studio working on some sketches. Iris and Oscar sat on the window seat watching people stroll past the shops on their way out for dinner or drinks or some shopping in the many boutiques and stores lining Main Street.

Nell loved to paint seascapes and beach scenes or pictures of sailing ships, but sometimes in the summer, she was drawn to creating shady woodland scenes, meadows full of wildflowers, or cool blue lakes tucked next to tall mountains.

She'd been working with pastels sketching out ideas and designs she would turn into oil paintings or watercolor pictures. Her run with Rob over the state park trails under the pines and deciduous trees had invigorated her and she was full of energy for the rest of the day.

Before settling to work in the studio, she'd taken the dogs to the beach where they ran and splashed and jumped in the waves returning home wet, sandy messes. Nell used the garden hose to rinse them down and both dogs had fun nipping at the stream of water pouring out of the hose.

Violet had gone to Boston to deliver some of her jewelry creations to a number of the shops on Newbury Street and in the Seaport district that carried her line of bracelets, necklaces, and earrings, and was now in the kitchen heating up a late supper.

Nell pinned some of the completed woodland drawings onto the bulletin board above her work station and then she started on the next composition moving the different shades of green pastels over the sketchbook page. She reached for several hues of yellow, tangerine, and light orange chalk pastel sticks and carefully incorporated the colors into the picture.

Next came a violet and a deep purple to add color next to some of the greens.

Nell was so engrossed in her work that she didn't hear Violet coming into the room with a tray, and she startled when she realized her sister was standing next to her.

Violet chuckled when Nell jumped. "You're really absorbed in what you're doing. I could have been a burglar and cleaned out the whole house and you wouldn't have even noticed." She set a cup of tea and a plate of cheese and crackers on Nell's desk and then pulled over a chair and started in on her dinner of lasagna and salad, telling her sister about her day in Boston. "I got a bunch of new orders. The store managers are very happy with the sales of my designs."

Nell congratulated Violet on her success and then told her about the mini-test of her skills Rob had her do in the university campus center.

"I think it's smart to take things day by day," Violet said. "Take part in the tests when you feel like it. If you become uneasy about things, then halt them. Work through it as you go. Rob will understand if you decide to discontinue the experiments into your abilities. You need to feel comfortable with what's going on."

Violet turned her attention to her sister's artwork. "Wow, you've done a lot of forest scenes. They're beautiful. The work is stunning. I see you've drawn quite a few views of the trees where Oscar became intent on something in the ticket."

Nell looked from picture to picture hanging on the bulletin board. "I didn't even realize I was drawing that same spot on the trail."

"It made quite an impression on you, I guess." Violet ate another bite of lasagna.

"I guess so." Nell stared at her drawings and was struck by the sparkling particles of yellows and whites she'd included in the pictures.

And for some reason, tiny shivers of anxiety pulsed down her spine every time she looked at them.

19

"We've received some information," Chief Lambert told Nell. "I won't say from who or from where, but the material is extremely sensitive and shouldn't be shared outside of this room. I'll give you an overview. I won't be able to answer your questions. A number of years ago, there was a trial to put away a mob boss. One of the witnesses had seen this boss execute several people, his sister among them."

Nell gasped. She knew the witness had to be Adam Timson.

"The crime ring was involved in moving stolen goods, artwork, antique jewelry, valuable things of that nature. The witness's sister had infiltrated the ring and had passed information out to law enforcement that would help put the boss away, but before she could get out, she was killed."

Nell felt her throat tighten.

"The witness was put into protection. As is often the case with crime rings such as this one, a new leader took over and after some time passed, the criminal activity ramped up once again. This is a very dangerous group. They're out to murder every person who testified against the boss including members of the ring who turned on them." The chief looked closely at Nell. "They're searching for the witness. These people are ruthless. They *will* kill him. Unless law enforcement can find him first."

Nell took a deep breath. "Is there anything I can do to help?"

"If there is, I'll call you. For now, you and your sister should clear your minds of Adam Timson. You don't know anything about him. You've had nothing to do with trying to find him. If anyone asks, all you know is that an officer asked you to take in some-one's dog."

"Okay." A chill ran over Nell's skin. "We can do that." She hesitated, but went ahead and asked the question. "Do you know where Adam Timson grew up?"

"I don't, and if I did know, I don't think I'd tell

you," Chief Lambert said. "In the near future, I might ask you to take a look at something, but you'll be in a vehicle with dark windows and when you move from the SUV to the place we'll be taking a look at, you will not be visible to anyone nearby."

"Okay." Nell felt like she was shrinking into herself.

"I'm sorry this is such a mess of a case."

"Don't be sorry. I entered into this thing of my own free will. If I didn't use my skills to help, well, it wouldn't be the right thing to do." Nell gave the chief a weak smile. "We can't let the bad guys win."

One corner of the chief's mouth turned up, and he gave Nell a solemn nod.

THE SUN WAS BEATING DOWN on Nell when she walked into the rear yard of her house and heard her neighbor, John Patrick, call from his porch. "How about a cold drink and a comfortable seat in the shade?"

"Sounds good to me." Nell wasn't surprised to see Iris and Oscar get up from the floor of John's porch to come and greet her. The dogs left the yard several times a day to visit with John and Ida while the sisters tended the shop or went out for a while.

John went inside and came out with a glass of seltzer with a slice of lime on the rim and handed it to Nell. They sat down in the white rockers.

"This is the perfect spot." Nell sipped her drink. "Shaded from the sun, flowers all around the yard, the ocean off in the distance, birds singing in the trees, and a friendly neighbor sitting beside me. It's just what I needed."

"Tough day?"

"Not so much tough. I'd call it depressing. I met with Chief Lambert. He found out some details about the trial that put Adam into witness protection. It wasn't an uplifting story."

"Dealing with criminals and the underbelly of society rarely is." John had been a journalist and was now retired from investigative reporting. He'd won many awards for his work including a Pulitzer and over the years, he'd been part of excellent news teams who broke and reported on important stories. John was proud of his work and often said he was happy he'd had a career that made him feel like he'd done some good.

"I bet you know this trial from years ago," Nell said. "I'm not allowed to say what it was about. I don't know most of it anyway, but what I heard was enough. I feel terribly for Adam. I hope he's okay and that he'll eventually contact the marshals' office for help."

John asked, "The police aren't close to locating him?"

"No. No one has a clue where he's gone."

John gave Oscar a pat on the head. "If this dog of his is any indication, Adam must be a good guy."

Iris got up and went to Nell pushing her snout under the young woman's hand to ask for some scratching. Nell obliged. "Imagine having your life upended like that? Leaving everything you know and becoming someone else? New name, new city, new friends. You must feel like an alien."

"Not to mention always looking over your shoulder," John said. "Always checking for danger, always being aware of your surroundings, having to be wary of others, never being able to tell people your story, having to lie about so many things. Don't ever slip up, don't make a mistake. All to keep you safe ... all to keep you alive."

"It would be a nightmare," Nell said. "I don't know if I could do it."

"If you wanted to live, you'd do it." John rocked slowly in his chair. "I knew of a couple of cases of witnesses in protection where the people didn't take it serious enough. One young guy had been settled in the Midwest. He decided, against the advice of the marshals, to return east in order to attend a funeral. He rented a car to use and the second day he was home, he got into the car, started the engine, and was blown to smithereens."

Nell let out a breath of air. "How awful."

"In the other case, a young woman had been in a gang," John told Nell. "The woman testified against some of the members and was placed in protection. She had a hard time adjusting to her new life. She ended up contacting a few old friends, they even went to visit her. She made the bad decision to go back to her old city for a visit. She was found beaten to death. She hadn't been home more than three days. The criminals in these cases don't forget, they don't let things go, they want revenge and will take it given the slightest opportunity. It can be a harsh world."

"Adam seems to have been a careful man. He'd been in protection for a while. His associates told us Adam didn't talk about himself, wouldn't go near crowds, preferred to be at home or with one or two friends. Actually, I'm not sure you could even call them friends. He didn't have a girlfriend. He didn't really date. He worked from home. Adam led a very quiet life." Nell took another swallow of her seltzer. "I wonder if he was lonely? I imagine he probably was."

"Not an easy way to live your life."

Ida came out to the porch with a dog treat for Iris and Oscar. "Why the long faces? You two having a serious discussion?"

Nell explained what they'd been talking about, and Ida nodded her head.

"A lot of people have very difficult lives," Ida said. "The resilient ones might adapt, but I believe they probably lose a tiny part of themselves along the way. I just don't know why things have to be so hard for so many people. I hope this missing young man can find his way to safety, and can make himself a happy life someday."

"Those are thoughtful wishes," Nell smiled. "Maybe they'll find their way to Adam and bring him good luck."

20

———

The new Colonial house stood on a manicured half-acre on the west side of Worcester in a tree-lined neighborhood of similar style houses. Nell pulled to the side of the road and the sisters stared at the home.

"It feels like a hundred years ago that we lived here," Violet said peering out the passenger side window. "They did a nice job building the new house. It fits the neighborhood. It looks a lot like our house used to."

Nell hadn't been back to the area since the tornado ripped through and destroyed their childhood home. Her breathing rate had sped up and she could feel beads of perspiration running down her back.

The neighborhood had recovered for the most part. Some trees had been planted where the older ones had been ripped from the ground, the houses that had been damaged or torn apart had been repaired or new ones built in their places, everything was neat and clean and well-tended. No one would believe such a wild, devastating storm could have hit the area ... no one but the people who lived through it.

"Are you okay?" Violet asked her sister.

Nell swallowed. "I'm okay, but it's sunny and pleasant today. If it was raining or stormy or windy, I might *not* be so okay." She let out a sigh. "It's strange to see a new house on the lot. It feels like our memories are playing a trick on us ... where's our house ... it's gone, but I know we used to live right here. It's almost as if we've been erased without a trace."

Violet nodded. "Sort of like Adam Timson and his old life."

Nell pulled away and drove down the streets to a different neighborhood on the other side of the city consisting of smaller, single family homes, duplexes, and three-deckers until they found the place they were looking for.

Adam's former address was a Cape-style house

set on a pretty lot with an accessory apartment extending to the side of the home. Flower boxes were set under all the windows and pots of blooms stood beside the front door.

An older man was trimming some bushes at the side of the property.

Nell and Violet got out of the car and approached the man hoping he was the homeowner.

"Good morning," Nell said with a smile.

The man turned towards them. He looked to be in his seventies, had white hair, pale blue eyes, and was slim and trim. "Hello. Can I help you with something?" He had a friendly voice and an easy-going demeanor.

Violet introduced herself and her sister. "We have an old friend we're trying to find. We heard he used to live here. Adam Timson."

"Oh, sure. Adam. He did live here, but he moved away about two and half years ago."

"Do you know where he went?" Nell asked.

"I don't. He was going to send me a postcard or a text to tell me his new address, but he never did. I guess he got busy and it slipped his mind."

"Did he stay in Massachusetts?" Violet asked the man.

"He said he might. Adam also said he wanted to drive around up north and see how it looked up there. He wanted a change. He's self-employed so it doesn't really matter where he lives. He's a free bird." The man smiled, and then he extended his hand. "Oh, I don't know where my manners went. I'm George. George Brown. How do you know Adam?"

Nell and Violet had rehearsed an answer in case that question came up. They didn't like telling the man a fib, but there wasn't really a way around it.

"We all lived in Boston for a short while. We met him there. It was years ago. We got to wondering where he was now."

"He's got a business website. Did you search on his name?"

"We did. The business website doesn't list an address around here. It's one of those addresses that handle business mail, collecting it and sending it on to the owner. Adam's email and phone number are on the website. We've sent a couple of emails and tried his phone, but we haven't got any replies." Nell smiled and kidded, "Maybe he doesn't want to renew the friendship."

"That can't be it," George said kindly. "Maybe Adam's closed the business and is starting something else."

"That could be," Violet agreed. "We were driving by the city and decided to stop and see if there was anyone around his old address who knew him."

"I knew him, but I'm no help in pointing you in his direction. Sorry about that." George took a handkerchief from his back pocket and dabbed at his forehead. "Adam's a popular guy. Someone else came by recently asking for him."

The little hairs on Nell's arms stood up. "Really?"

"Who was it? An old friend?" Violet kept her voice even, not wanting to show any alarm that someone had come looking for Adam.

"He didn't give his name. Sort of looked like a tough guy."

"A tough guy?" Nell questioned.

"Not a criminal or anything. I mean someone who worked out a lot, a macho kind of guy. He was dressed well, nice shirt and slacks, looked expensive. Seemed he had some money."

"How old was he?"

"Mid-thirties?"

"Did he say why he was looking for Adam?" Nell asked.

"He told me they'd gone to school together." George shrugged.

"Did he say anything else?"

"He just asked where Adam had moved to. I told the guy he could give me his name and contact information and if Adam ever got in touch with me, I'd pass it on to him. The guy declined." George said, "I'd be happy to do the same for you if you'd like to leave your email or number."

"That's very nice of you." Violet took a pen and a small piece of paper from her bag and gave George their information thinking he would find it odd if they didn't accept his offer.

"What did you think of Adam?" Nell asked.

"What a great tenant. A pleasant man, always paid on time, kept the apartment immaculate, was quiet. We hardly knew he was there."

"Does he have a partner?"

"Not to my knowledge. I never saw a girlfriend or anyone visiting him. We assumed Adam liked his privacy. The apartment is small so we just figured he preferred to meet friends or his date somewhere else to socialize."

"He worked out of the apartment?" Nell asked.

"He did most of the time. He worked at the library, too. Adam didn't meet his clients here. The parking is limited and like I said, the apartment is quite small."

"Did he have any pets when he lived here?"

George's eyes lit up. "He had a dog, Oscar. A brown, mixed-breed. A fine animal. Adam brought the dog here for us to meet before he signed the lease so we could see what a good dog he was. My wife and I fell in love with Oscar." George chuckled. "We told Adam that Oscar was the only reason we rented to him."

"Did Adam say where he lived before he moved into this apartment?"

"I don't recall anything specific. Adam paid us six months in advance so we didn't bother running a credit check on him. He told us he'd moved around the state. He did tell me he'd love a place near the ocean someday."

"Did he ever mention any family members?"

"He said his parents had passed away and that he had a sister, but she died. I think he was on his own. No family ever showed up to visit. Oscar is his family. The guy loves that dog, and that dog loves him."

The sisters thanked George for talking with them and when they returned to the car, Violet asked, "So who was the guy who showed up recently looking for Adam?"

"It couldn't have been a U.S. Marshal. The protection program knew Adam was living in Saxonwood so I'm going to guess it was one of the bad guys. It sounded like he came asking questions right around the time of the photo exhibition. Thankfully, Adam never told George where he'd moved to. There must have been a reason Adam left here and moved to the North Shore."

Violet said, "Maybe the only reason was he wanted to be closer to the ocean and asked permission to move an hour to the north. We'll never know for sure. No marshal would give that information to anyone and even if we meet Adam someday, I'm positive he isn't allowed to talk about where he's lived and why the location was chosen."

"Anyway, the criminal must have found out Adam had lived here prior to moving to Saxonwood. He took the chance of coming here and asking the landlord if he had a following address for Adam. They know he must be living in the Bluewater area. The photo in the exhibit listed Bluewater Cove beach in the title of the picture."

"What a mess." Violet sat up in her seat. "Bonnie Plant's name is listed as the photographer on the photos in the exhibit. Why haven't the criminals found her and forced her to tell them where Adam is living?"

Nell gave her sister a look of concern. "Maybe they found out on their own. We need to talk to Chief Lambert."

21

Nell rang the doorbell while holding a basket of goodies she and Violet put together for Adam's neighbor, Scott McKenzie. The gift basket held boxes of tea, bars of premium chocolate, a package of gourmet popcorn, butter biscuits, lemon cookies, and an assortment of blueberry, corn, and cinnamon muffins.

Scott's wife, Sheryl, opened the door and her face showed surprise from seeing Nell on her doorstep.

"Nell. It's so nice to see you."

"Violet had to watch the store, but we wanted to drop off a get-well basket for Scott. We heard he'd come home recently and we want to wish him a speedy recovery."

"That's very thoughtful. Come in and have a seat. How about a cup of tea?" Sheryl held the door open for the young woman.

"Oh, I don't want to intrude," Nell protested. "Scott must need to rest."

"Scott isn't home. He's been sent to rehab for a few weeks. He isn't quite ready to be home until he's stronger. I'd love to have you stay for tea. I've been sort of anxious about the whole experience. Do you have time to come in for a little while?"

Nell agreed and they went into the big, recently-renovated kitchen where Sheryl made tea and put out some cookies while Nell took a seat at the center island.

"This incident has really made me aware of how easy it is for disaster to strike." Sheryl took mugs from the cabinet. "Thank the heavens Scott will be fine, but he'll have a long recovery. A split second decision can lead to a whole lot of trouble. The hand of fate can reach out and grab you at any moment. The thought of how easy we can swing from normal, everyday living to a near-death accident has me shaken. I'm feeling vulnerable and distressed and I haven't been able to throw it off."

"Do you think speaking with a counselor would help?" Nell added a little milk to her tea.

"I've made an appointment. I figure it can't hurt." Sheryl placed some napkins on the counter.

"How is Scott doing?" Nell asked. "Is he feeling the same way?"

Sheryl stirred a teaspoon of sugar into her tea. "He's been talking with someone at the rehab place. Initially, he was thankful to be alive, then he became discouraged that the recovery would be so slow, but now he's feeling more realistic about his recovery and understands things take time and he needs to be patient."

"Good for him. It sounds like he's handling things well."

"I keep reliving that night." Sheryl looked down at her mug and shook her head. "I'm in the sunroom at the back of the house. For a few seconds, Scott sees the light on in Adam's place and then it goes out. He decides to go check. He wanted to see if Adam was back and if he was okay. I guess as he was crossing the lawn, Scott wondered if someone had broken into Adam's house, but he decided to have a look and then call the police if necessary." Sheryl pushed at her blond bangs. "He didn't get the chance."

"You heard the gunshot?" Nell asked.

"I did." Sheryl's voice sounded shaky. "I jumped

to my feet and listened. Did a car backfire? Was the sound caused by a tire blowing out as a car went by on the street? My heart was pounding." The woman unconsciously moved her hand to her chest. "I stepped outside and called Scott's name. There was no answer. I walked closer to Adam's house and called again. Still no answer. I kept my eyes on the windows to see if a light came on and I edged over to the garage. That's when I saw Scott lying on his back in the driveway. He wasn't moving. I honestly almost died right there."

"You called the police?" Nell asked.

"I had my phone with me. I ran to Scott. He was bleeding, but he was alive. I don't even remember calling the police. My mind seemed to switch to autopilot. I don't recall much of what happened after the emergency people arrived. I do remember thinking it was taking them so long to come. It felt like an eternity."

"Did you do something to stop the bleeding?" Nell held her mug in her hand.

"I had a sweater on. I took it off and bunched it up and pressed it against the wound." Sheryl's eyes filled up. "I wasn't sure if it was the right thing to do. I just did it because it came into my head that I needed to stop the flow of blood."

"You did the right thing," Nell nodded to Sheryl with a warm smile. "It was lucky you were at home and reacted the way you did."

"How I wish I'd told Scott to stay in the house and not go over to Adam's place. If Adam had indeed returned home, Scott could have seen him in the morning. If it was a burglar, well, if we'd thought of that possibility, then Scott shouldn't have gone over there at all." Sheryl sighed. "Live and learn. My stomach feels sick whenever I think of what could have happened."

"But it didn't happen." Nell spoke with a kind, supportive tone. "Scott will be home soon. He'll be feeling fine before you know it."

"I'm so grateful." Sheryl's eyes looked tired.

"Did Scott get a look at the person who fired on him?" Nell asked.

"He didn't." Sheryl took a deep breath to try to release some of the tension she was feeling. "Scott said the garage door was open. He saw a flash, and that was it. He can't remember anything else. He woke up in the hospital trying to figure out what had happened to bring him there."

"Does Scott have any idea if the shooter was a man or a woman?"

"He can't be sure. His mind is a muddle about

the incident," Sheryl said. "The police interviewed Scott, but he wasn't able to give a description of the gunman. It happened so fast, he didn't notice the kitchen door into the garage open. All he recalls is the gun's bright, red flash ... and then nothing. Scott told me he had a half-second memory where he wondered if someone had shot at him. He doesn't recall being hit or anything after that. I'm sure that's a blessing. He only has the vaguest recollection that I was kneeling next to him. Scott thought it might have been a dream."

"Does Scott remember hearing any sounds that night?" Nell asked. "Like the sound of the kitchen door opening? Maybe the blast of the gun as it went off? Did the gunman yell anything to him?"

"Scott hasn't mentioned hearing anything," Sheryl told the young woman. "At least, he didn't tell me he heard anything."

"Did he notice a car parked near the house?"

Sheryl shook her head again. "For Scott, it's like the minutes before the gun fired and the hours after the shooting never existed. He doesn't remember."

"What about you?" Nell questioned. "Did you notice a car parked in front of the house or close by? Did you see anyone trying to flee?"

Sheryl thought hard about the questions. "I don't

think so. It was dark. I was frightened by the sound of the gunshot. I was in panic mode, especially after I found Scott collapsed in the driveway, bleeding. It was a nightmare. I don't know how I didn't faint dead-away right then and there. I did faint later on," Sheryl admitted.

An idea came to Nell. "Have you seen anyone around Adam's house since he's taken off?"

Sheryl nodded. "I saw the mail carrier. I told him Adam had gone away for a while and that maybe he should put a hold on delivering to Adam's house until he reported to them he'd returned."

"Good idea. Did anyone else come by? Any deliveries that you noticed?"

"No." Sheryl's eyes widened slightly. "Oh, there was a man from the gas company there one day. I was outside working on the flower garden. I saw him walking around Adam's house a few times like he was looking for something. I went over and told him Adam was at work and asked if there something I could answer for him. I didn't want him to know Adam had left town. He seemed brusque. He said he was doing an inspection. I asked him what he was inspecting. He gave me such a dirty look."

"Did he answer your question?" Nell asked.

"He said he was inspecting the propane gas

tank." Sheryl looked annoyed recalling her exchange with the gas man. "I thought he was rude."

"Was he wearing a uniform?"

"He had on jeans and a worker's shirt with the company name written on it."

"What company did he work for?" Nell questioned.

Sheryl frowned. "I don't remember what it said."

"Do you heat with gas?"

"Gas isn't available for heating in this neighborhood. The house is heated with oil. We have a gas range though so we have a propane tank for that."

"What's the name of the company you use?" Nell asked.

"Evergreen," Sheryl said.

"Was that the name on the man's shirt?"

"It was something else." Sheryl's lips tightened as she thought. "Oh, it was Country Gas. That was it."

"I wonder why he was doing an inspection?" Nell tapped on her phone searching on the name. "I can't find the company. Nothing comes up."

"I'm sure it was Country Gas. I remember thinking it said *County* Gas. I was concerned that the town was having issues with propane gas tanks and was having a county government official inspecting the tanks. Then I realized it said *country*." Suddenly,

Sheryl gave Nell a look. "You can't find the company listing?"

Nell shook her head, and then her expression became one of concern. "Maybe it isn't a legitimate company."

"He wasn't a representative of a gas company at all, was he?" Sheryl's face paled. "He must have been looking for Adam."

"You saw the man up close," Nell said excitedly. "Tell Chief Lambert. Give him the man's description. Then the officers in the area can be on the lookout for him."

22

"I don't know why I'm so nervous." Watching the streetlights go by as they sped along the dark streets of Saxonwood, Nell sat in the backseat of a big black SUV with Violet at her side.

"Probably because of all this cloak and dagger stuff." Violet looked out through the windshield. "Isn't it more suspicious to have two black SUVs with tinted windows driving up to Adam Timson's house than regular cars? It's like some dignitary arriving somewhere with police protection. This calls attention to us."

The officer who was driving said, "I'm going to pull into the garage and when the door goes down, then you can get out, but please don't leave the vehicle before the door closes."

Violet looked at her sister. "See? No wonder you feel nervous. Everything about this visit is designed to strike fear into your heart."

Nell had the urge to chuckle at Violet's comments, but her throat was so tight and dry that the laugh got stuck and couldn't make it out.

The SUV drove backwards up Adam's driveway and slipped into the garage with the front of the vehicle facing out. With a mechanical grinding noise, the door slowly came down and stopped with a thud.

"All set," the driver said cheerfully. "I'll be right here in the car when you're ready to leave."

When Nell and Violet got out, the kitchen door leading into the garage opened and Chief Lambert and Peter came out to greet the sisters.

"We made it here in one piece." Nell tried to make light of the tension everyone was feeling.

"I was hoping you would," Chief Lambert gave a quick smile and then led them into the house.

At Nell's, Violet's, and Peter's suggestion, the chief had made arrangements with the Saxonwood police for the four of them to tour Adam Timson's house one more time.

"Is there something in particular you're looking for?" the chief asked.

"We think we may have overlooked something when we were here before," Violet explained. "When we here looking through the trash and found a receipt for things to use in a disguise, what happened to the rest of the trash?"

"A few officers went through it," the chief said, his bald head reflecting the light of the overhead recessed lights. "Nothing of importance was found."

"It makes sense." Nell walked around the kitchen opening the drawers and the cabinet doors. "People in protection must be taught not to leave notes or phone numbers lying around the house or thrown in the trash that might compromise their safety. Adam got a little sloppy when he tossed out the receipt listing all the things he bought to change his appearance."

"Luckily you found the receipt before someone broke into the house and discovered it," Chief Lambert said. "We arrived a little ahead of you," he told the sisters. "We made a search around the doors and in the garage looking for anything that might indicate an explosive device had been set up that would trigger and go off if Adam came back home."

Nell swallowed hard. "I guess you didn't find anything?"

"We gave it the all clear," Peter informed them. "It's safe to inspect the rooms."

Chief Lambert told the sisters, "In answer to the question you asked this morning about Bonnie Plant, she *was* visited by an *old friend* of Adam's who asked if she could give him Adam's address. This happened right after Adam left town. Bonnie was happy to give the address to the man and she told him Adam had gone away for a while."

"Thankfully, Adam had run away by then," Nell said.

When Peter and the chief left the kitchen area and went to look around the living room, Violet sidled up to her sister. "What are you looking for in here?"

Nell shrugged. "Anything. Some little clue. I don't know what it might be, but maybe we'll know it if we find something."

Violet started on the other side of the kitchen going through the drawers and cabinetry. "A lot of these drawers are nearly empty."

"I suppose if you know you might have to flee at the drop off a hat, you learn to live with less," Nell suggested.

"We should learn to live with less," Violet decided. "We have too much clutter. Imagine how our house will look in ten years? We won't be able to move in the basement at all."

"Nothing important in here." Nell closed the last cabinet door.

"Can you still see colors on the walls?" Violet questioned.

"Not much. A little residue here and there. Most of the color has disappeared."

"Like Adam. Gone without a trace, and nobody knows to where."

When Nell suggested they head to the basement, Violet agreed, but said, "You could eat dinner off the basement floor in this house. There's nothing down there."

"Let's look anyway."

The sisters went in opposite directions when they reached the bottom of the stairs, and each checked around the foundation, near the basement windows, all around the edges of the door leading to the outside, and up near the ceiling where beams crossed to support the floor above.

Nell pulled over a step ladder and pushed it against the cellar wall, then climbed up to check the space in between the top of the basement walls and the wood leading up to the first floor. She ran her hand over the rough cement of the wall and came away with only a bit of dust. Nell moved the ladder around the basement walls, each time climbing up and searching the nooks and crannies. At the last corner, she noticed a piece of paper stuck into one of the beams, and reaching for it, she pulled out an envelope.

"Violet. I found something." Nell handed the envelope to her sister and climbed down.

"A few pictures of Adam and Oscar." Violet handed one to her sister.

"Adam took some pictures of himself and Oscar on the beach. The sun's going down." Nell held a photo of Adam with his arm around Oscar, the two of them looking into the camera. "They look happy."

There was one other photo of the man and his dog, and two more showing Oscar running along the wide stretch of wet sand chasing a Frisbee. Nell's heart contracted with sadness.

"Adam hid these here," Violet said. "I bet he forgot them in his haste."

"He probably printed these few pictures to have if he ever had to run," Nell surmised. "If he had to run, he knew he'd have to destroy his phone and all the pictures he'd taken would be lost."

"Most likely, Adam didn't have *any* photos on his phone," Violet said. "He probably took very few, printed some, and then deleted them from his phone. No trace, be safe."

Nell nodded, still looking at the small photos in her hand. "Adam looks like he really loves Oscar." Her voice was soft. "So sad to have to leave him behind."

Violet let out a sigh before saying, "Come on. Let's show the pictures to Peter and Chief Lambert."

When they reached the top of the stairs, Violet called to the men and Peter replied from the garage. "We're out here."

The sisters walked through the kitchen and went down the three steps into the two-car garage to see Peter at the top of the ladder that led to the storage space over the car bays.

Violet handed the photos to the chief and told him where Nell found them.

"It seems the guy sure loved that dog," the chief said while flipping through the pictures. "There's nothing in these pictures to reveal who Adam is or even where they are. Could be any beach. Even so, he didn't leave the photos hanging around the house. Good. He was careful."

Peter climbed down the steps of the pull-down ladder. "You want to take a look?" he asked Nell.

"The space looks the same to me, but another set of eyes never hurts."

Nell made eye contact with the chief. "Do you want to have a look?"

"I went up already," Chief Lambert said. "Why don't you take a quick look."

Nell climbed the wobbly steps and had to crouch a little from the low ceiling when she moved onto the plywood floor of the storage space from the top step. She walked around gingerly looking for anything important they might have missed the last time they were there.

The sports equipment stood against the wall. A pair of snowshoes, some skis, some cross country skis and a few poles. Nothing else. They hadn't overlooked anything on their last visit. Nell started back to the steps, and just as she turned around to begin backing down the staircase, she stopped.

She let her eyes rove over the storage space, and then she knew what was bothering her. Hurriedly, she hustled down the steps.

"Up there." Nell pointed, her breath coming quick and shallow. "The sports equipment."

"What about it?" Peter asked.

"The camping gear." Nell's voice held a tinge of excitement. "It's gone."

Violet's eyes widened and Peter tore up the steps to the storage space. He called down to them. "Nell's right. That stuff is gone."

Chief Lambert scratched the back of his neck, his mind racing.

"He came back," Nell said, her voice breathless. "Adam came back."

Violet looked confused.

"He came back for the gear." A smile crossed Nell's face. "Adam didn't leave the area. He's still around. He's camping in the woods. He must be in the state park."

"He's afraid to go to one of the marshals's offices," Violet said. "He's keeping out of sight until he feels it's safe to contact the protection program."

Chief Lambert smiled. "Well, since we know where Adam might be, maybe we can actually find him now ... before someone dangerous finds him first."

23

The police sent two pairs of officers into the woods to look for Adam Timson. They dressed as hikers and spent five hours on three different days searching various sections of the forest without success. Chief Lambert contacted the Boston office of the U.S. Marshals to inform them of the idea Adam might be hiding in the state park.

Violet and Nell weren't surprised to hear the news. The state park covered a little more than a thousand acres of woodland and if Adam heard two men approaching, he would surely hide from them. They didn't think Adam would be more likely to interact with men dressed as police officers since you could purchase an official-looking uniform on the internet, and he wouldn't trust the fact they were real officers and not the people out to kill him.

"What do you think should be done?" Violet asked her sister as the two worked in the studio with Nell painting and Violet creating some prototypes of her new jewelry designs.

Nell replied without looking up from her painting. "I don't know if there's anything else that can be done. If the police take a helicopter over the park looking for Adam, he'll hide. He's not going to trust anyone. Keeping himself safe is the main goal. He won't take a chance interacting with anyone. I'd do the same. I'd wait until time passed and then I'd try to contact a marshal."

"It makes sense." Violet spread some gemstones on the felt mat in front of her. "But Adam needs to be found before one of the criminals gets to him." She looked up from her work with an expression of horror. "What if they've already found him?"

"Oh, no." Nell didn't know why they hadn't yet thought of that possibility. Maybe Chief Lambert had, but he didn't say a word about it to them. Adam could be dead. The criminals might have hidden his body somewhere remote in the forest. Somewhere, it would take a very long time to find.

Waves of anxiety pulsed through Nell's body. They'd been too slow to figure out where Adam had fled to ... but now, even though they had a good idea he was hiding in the state park, the man was still elusive.

"I don't think there's anything that can be done." Nell put down her paintbrush. "If he's still alive, Adam will have to find his way to communicate with the protection program. He'll do everything in his power to keep from being found. The police can't use their resources looking for Adam every day. They'll have to give up."

Iris and Oscar trotted into the room and greeted the young women.

"You want to go out?" Nell patted the friendly, wiggling animals. "Why don't we take a break before we make dinner and sit outside in the yard for a while?" she asked her sister.

"Good idea." Violet stood up from her stool. "I could use some fresh air."

Nell glanced over at her sister. "I just thought of someone Adam *would* trust."

Violet tilted her head to the side not understanding her sister's meaning. "Who?"

Nell smiled, turned her head, and looked at Oscar.

Oh," Violet said. "Why didn't we think of this before?"

WHEN NELL, Violet, and the two dogs got out of the car after parking in the tiny dirt lot near the trails, Nell glanced up at the sky and her body went weak.

"Is it supposed to storm this evening?" she asked Violet.

"Maybe some light showers later. Nothing to be concerned about."

The dogs galloped off down the trail and the sisters followed after them carrying the leashes.

Violet said, "When we reach the spot where Oscar was whining and staring into the woods, we'll encourage him to find Adam and we'll go the way the dog goes."

"Right. It's a long shot, but what else can we do? Oscar is the only living thing Adam will trust and if he sees us with the dog, maybe he'll trust us, too."

They walked for thirty minutes, and when they arrived at the thicket, Nell led the dogs off the trail and into the woods. She knelt next to Oscar and patted his head. "Adam needs you, boy. Can you go find Adam? Where's Adam?"

Oscar wagged his tail, turned around in a circle, and barked.

Nell stood and gestured into the woods. "Go find Adam, Oscar. Go get Adam."

The dog barked and whirled around. He hurried through the brush with Iris and the sisters dashing after him.

It was tough going ... the young women's legs got twisted up in long vines, they had to push past low-growing branches and bushes, and some of the terrain was slippery from small rocks underfoot. Several times, they had to call to the dogs to make them stop until they could catch up.

Nell had some scratches on her face and Violet's ponytail had some pieces of green leaves stuck in it. Perspiration clung to their backs and showed on their foreheads.

"I thought I was in pretty good shape," Nell groaned.

"No one can keep up with a couple of dogs." Violet huffed as they climbed a steep hill. "Finally, there's a trail up ahead. Oscar and Iris are following it."

At the top of the hill, they stopped to catch their breaths.

"Adam could be anywhere." Violet sucked in a

long breath. "Oscar might just be running through the woods for fun. He might not have Adam's scent at all. Do you think we should go back? It's going to be dark soon."

"When we first started out, Oscar was sniffing all over the ground in the thicket he was staring into that day we walked on the trail. There was a scent in that thicket and he found it. Maybe it's not Adam's scent. Maybe it's the smell of a deer or some other animal."

Violet interrupted. "It better not be a bear."

"Whatever it is, Oscar is after it. Remember I saw the yellow and white colors in the thicket ... the yellow and white particles glowing in the air? They were still there when we went back a few days after I first saw them. They were slightly faded, but they were still there. Those colors mean joy, love, simple sacred things. I think Adam saw Oscar with us. I think he hid, watching us. I think Adam left behind those feelings ... joy and love at seeing Oscar again, happiness at seeing that his dog was okay. The true, deep connection Adam has with his dog floated on the air in sparkling colors."

Nell reached into her backpack of supplies, removed two flashlights, and handed one to her sister. A gust of wind blew over the young women lifting their hair from their shoulders for a few seconds. Nell looked up at the sky, but it was hard to see through all the branches and leaves. For a second, she shuddered, afraid that a storm was brewing. The air smelled like rain. The wind was picking up. *I'll be okay. It will only be a shower. I'll be okay.*

"I think we should keep going. For a little longer anyway." Nell zipped up her backpack and slung it over her shoulder.

"Okay. I'm not ready to give up. Yet." Violet gave her sister a half-smile. "Let's go find the dogs."

After walking for another thirty-five minutes, Violet stopped. "I'm exhausted. It will be fully dark out soon and it's hard to see even with this big flashlight. We need to turn back. It will take us a long time to get to the car."

Nell sighed. "You're right." She called to Iris and Oscar.

"They got ahead of us," Violet said, and she called the dogs' names. "Oh, man. Where are they?"

A light shower started to fall.

Suddenly, Oscar's bark cut through the air, followed by Iris's howl.

And then, the sound of a gunshot ricocheted through the woods.

Violet grabbed her sister's arm.

Off in the distance, the dogs barked like wild animals.

Nell removed her phone from her pocket and moaned. "No service. Come on, let's walk slow and quiet. Flick off the flashlights. We'll have a look," she whispered. "I don't want to leave the dogs behind."

They moved softly along the trail heading towards the sound of the barking dogs when Iris came charging down the path and almost crashed into them. She barked and whirled, looked back at them, and took off. Nell and Violet ran after her.

Iris ran off the trail and onto a smaller one, then veered to the left and stopped.

A man was on his back. Oscar stood over him. When he saw the women, he whined.

Nell took small steps forward. Red color swirled all around in the growing darkness. She shined her flashlight onto the man.

Adam Timson. He opened his eyes and used his arm to shade them from the flashlight.

"Adam?" Nell moved closer. "Are you okay? I'm Ellen Finley. My sister, Violet, is here with me. We've been taking care of Oscar."

When Adam saw the dog, he pushed himself up slightly as tears fell from his eyes. "Oscar," he whispered, and then he groaned in pain. Adam put his arm around his dog. "I've been shot. In my thigh."

Nell dropped her backpack and pulled out the first aid kit.

"Who shot you?" Violet's voice was panicked. "Where is he?"

When Adam slumped onto his back, Oscar licked his face.

"Where's the gunman?" Violet demanded. "Is he nearby?"

"Point the flashlight on his leg," Nell told her sister as she used a small jackknife to cut at the man's pant leg. Blood was all over his jeans.

"You know who I am?" Adam asked hoarsely. He kept his hand on Oscar's back.

"We know." Nell worked to stop the flow of blood.

"Did the gunman run away?" Violet asked.

"No," Adam told them. "I think I killed him."

Violet let out a gasp.

"I shot him. He was trying to kill me. My gun's right here. Take it. In case another one of them comes for me." Adam pushed it towards Violet. "I don't feel so good."

"Oh crap." Violet reached for the gun and held it like it was a dead fish. "Is there a second man?"

"I think so. I heard the guy's walkie-talkie squawk. He was communicating with someone." Adam looked up at Oscar's face and then he whispered to the sisters, "Take the gun. Get out of here. Take Oscar with you. Please don't let anything happen to him." Tears streamed down the man's face.

Nell pulled off her sweater, twisted it up into a long roll, then pushed it under and around Adam's leg wound to try and slow the bleeding. She used the knife to cut the cords off the backpack and then used them to tie a tourniquet around the man's upper leg.

"You're going to need to help us," Nell told him. "You're going to have to stand up."

"I can't." Adam's face contorted in pain.

"You have to ... unless you want to die here. Now put your arm around my shoulders. Help me get him up," she told her sister.

Adam cried out as he was helped to his feet.

"Don't put pressure on the wounded leg. Use me and Violet to lean on. Let's go. We are not waiting around for some other criminal with a gun to come for us."

"I won't make it," Adam's words choked in his throat.

"You definitely won't make it if you stay here.

Now let's do this." Nell put her arm around the man's waist, and the three of them hobbled towards the trail, and as soon as they stepped onto the path, lightning flashed in the distance, thunder roared, and the heaven's opened with pelting rain ... and Nell almost collapsed to the ground.

24

"You'll be okay," Violet yelled to her sister over the noise of the thunder and the rain. "Keep walking. Don't stop, Nell. You're going to be okay. We're all going to be okay."

The next thing Violet shouted at her gave Nell something to hold on to.

"Focus on Adam."

Shaking like a leaf and feeling like she might become physically ill, Nell grabbed at the words her sister had said and repeated them over and over as they trudged along the dark path. *Focus on Adam.*

The dogs were in front walking slowly so they wouldn't get ahead of the humans.

The downpour came in torrents as the wind whipped through the trees, and every few seconds,

Nell, her tears mingling with the heavy drops of rain, whimpered wanting only to run or crawl away and hide under the brush.

Adam stopped. His weight was heavy on the sisters' shoulders and his head lolled to the side.

"Adam." Violet shook his arm afraid he'd passed away as they tried to move him from the place he'd encountered the gunman. "Adam."

The man groaned.

"Ease him to the ground." Violet gestured with her hand, and they slowly let Adam down onto the muddy trail so she could check his bleeding.

Nell crouched beside him, hunched over and held her head as lightning struck a tree near them with a mighty boom.

Yanking her sister to her feet, Violet shouted at Nell like a drill sergeant. "Nell. Get up. Adam is too weak to walk. Take his arms. I'll take his legs. We need to move him off the trail. One of us will stay with him, the other will run down the trail until there's cell service. Do you want to stay or go?"

"You're faster. You go."

Violet removed Adam's gun from the waistband of her jeans. "Take the gun."

"I don't know how to fire a gun," Nell nearly wailed.

"Hopefully, you won't have to figure out how to use it."

The women hauled the man off the trail about ten yards into the woods and hid him under the brush.

Violet took her sister's face in her hands. "The storm is almost over. It's not going to hurt you." Her voice broke when she gave her sister a hug and said, "If someone comes for Adam, don't fight back. Run."

Nell gave a weak smile. "I can't do that."

Violet's lips trembled.

"Go," Nell told her sister. "And get your butt back here as fast as you can."

And with a dog on each side of her, Nell sat down next to Adam holding the gun in her shaking hand.

"Take care of Nell and Adam," Violet spoke to the dogs with a husky voice and then she whirled and tore down the trail in the rain.

Nell pulled her legs up close, wrapped her arms around them, and began to rock slowly back and forth, feeling oh, so alone.

Oscar licked her cheek, and then he moved next to Adam, nuzzled the man with his snout, and lay down alongside him on the soaked and muddy ground.

Nell's heart melted at the sight of the dog's devotion and a sudden surge of rage at the gunman raced through her veins as she slid over the dirt towards Adam. Pushing his wet hair back from his forehead, she brushed her hand gently over his skin hoping the gentle contact would somehow soothe the unconscious man.

Nell checked his pulse. *Don't you die on us, Adam. Don't you die.*

The rain slowed to a shower, and the clouds raced overhead occasionally allowing the moonlight to shine down on them. Shivering and drenched, Nell held the gun in her hands pointing it in the direction they'd come from, hoping the torrential rain had washed away any traces of their shoes on the trails.

Nell looked at Adam's face smeared with blood and soil and her heart contracted thinking how the man had been alone for so many years hiding in plain sight, having to lie about his background, living on his own ... all to stay alive.

You're not alone now. I promise we won't leave you.

Sitting still as a stone, Nell watched the dark trail listening for footsteps, the skitter of a loose pebble, or the movement of a branch ... her heart pounding so hard she was sure everyone in Bluewater must be able to hear it.

And then Iris lifted her head and Nell's heart stood still.

Raising her hand, she held it palm out towards the dogs and shook her head indicating they should remain quiet and not move.

Oscar followed Iris's gaze and his nose twitched as he sniffed the air.

Nell forced herself to take in slow breaths trying to keep herself from passing out.

Time crawled by ... no one came looking for Adam.

Nell rested on her back. She might have dozed. She had no idea how long they'd been there. She checked Adam's pulse. It was weak, but his heart was beating.

The clouds had disappeared and the moonlight filtered through the branches and dappled the ground. The forest looked strange ... the colors glowed and shimmered, the atoms pulsed and moved like ocean waves over the air ... blues, greens, reds, and then a huge flash of orange on the trail. *Warning. Danger.*

Nell held her breath, and then she heard him, and in less than three seconds ... there he was.

A tall man. His clothes looked black, but it was hard to tell in the dark. She couldn't make out his face, but she could see that he held a gun ... a weapon that looked like a machine gun.

Alarmed, the dogs turned to look at Nell and she shook her head. They remained silent, but pinned their eyes to the enemy.

The man stepped slowly and deliberately, his head moving from side to side, listening, watching.

Nell sat like a statue. *Don't breathe. Don't move.* Her eyes were glued on the man. *Don't look over here.*

Hurried footsteps. More than one person. Coming from the other side of the trail.

Violet. They're going to come right up in front of the man.

Nell yanked off her shoe and tossed it in the direction away from where her sister was coming from.

The tall man whirled and crouched. His gun flashed and the explosive blast of it pained Nell's ears.

Oscar rushed to lay over Adam covering him as best he could.

The man on the trail saw the dog's movement. He quickly turned to aim at them.

Several cracks filled the air.

The man crumpled.

"Nell!" Violet's voice ripped through the air and Nell's heart leapt with joy.

Afraid the man might be faking his fall, Nell sat still, one hand on Iris, deciding if she should respond to her sister.

Two men raced up the trail. Officers.

"We're here," she yelled to them, and when she stood, Iris barked and barked.

"Nell?" Peter's voice called to her.

"It's me. We're here. Adam needs help."

In a rush, Violet, Chief Lambert, several other officers, and two EMTs darted into the woods towards Nell.

Violet wrapped her arms around her sister and sobbed as the medical personnel tended to the injured man and the chief used his handheld radio to call for a stretcher.

The next few hours were a blur. Nell and the dogs, despite Oscar's protests from having to leave Adam, were escorted down the hills to a waiting police SUV, Adam was taken to the hospital, and much later, the dead man with the gun and the man Adam shot in the woods were eventually put on stretchers and taken to the medical examiner's office for processing.

Exhausted, soaked to the bone, and covered with dirt, Nell, Violet, and the dogs sat quietly in the SUV and as they pulled away from the state park, Nell watched the white glowing particles of color dance all over Oscar's fur.

25

The two men who died trying to kill Adam Timson were identified and law enforcement worked to trace back who was responsible for sending them out on the hit.

Adam survived his gunshot wound and would soon be ready for his entry once again into protective custody in a new location.

Despite their protests, Nell and Violet had been taken to the hospital to be checked for hypothermia and dehydration, were treated and released that night. The dogs were brought to a vet for a health evaluation and were deemed to be strong and well.

Nell, Violet, Iris, and Oscar returned to their home just before dawn and although the dogs fell right to sleep, Nell and Violet were unable to rest and stayed awake until midnight the following night when they both stumbled into bed completely exhausted.

For weeks, Nell continued to have trouble sleeping and often woke up in terror soaked in a cold sweat. Her fear of storms had become worse, aggravated by the terrifying incident in the forested hills, and for almost a month, she was unable to run on the wooded trails of the state park with Rob.

Rob had shown up with a bouquet of white flowers for Nell and a mixed color bouquet for Violet. "Putting yourselves in danger has to stop," he admonished them. "You can't place your lives at risk. You're just ordinary people ... well, sort of ordinary. The police can't expect you to place yourselves in danger." He went on and on until Nell gently explained that they hadn't expected to run into such trouble in the woods.

"You need to be more forward-thinking," Rob grumped. "Don't be so naïve. The world can be a very dangerous place."

Nell was deeply touched by the man's concern, but she kidded him anyway. "You just don't want anything to happen to me because then your visual stimuli experiments will be out the window and you won't have anything to do until you find another tetrachromat to do your research on."

Rob was about to raise an objection when he realized Nell was teasing him. "Fine. Next time, when you're up to your eyeballs in danger, don't say I didn't try to warn you. And I won't be bringing you flowers the next time you have a lapse in judgment."

With Rob's kind attention and patience, eventually Nell was able to return to the state park to run with him.

"One foot in front of the other," he'd told her. "Small steps will lead you to your goal and before you know it, you'll have accomplished what you wanted to."

Nell didn't always tell him so, but she was very grateful to have Rob around.

Twice a week for the past two weeks, she and Violet had been taking the self-defense class Rob suggested to them and they both felt it was more than worthwhile.

"I hate to say it," Nell told her sister, "but it might not be a bad idea for us to take a gun safety class and learn how to shoot. If that guy in the woods had come at me with his weapon, I wouldn't have been able to fire Adam's gun to protect myself. I don't want to own a weapon, but it could save our lives someday if we learn how to handle a gun."

With a reluctant sigh, Violet agreed. "If you're going to keep helping the police, it's probably a good idea."

NELL AND VIOLET, sitting nervously in the back of a black SUV, rode through the streets of Boston to a large warehouse building. One of the silver metal doors rose and the vehicle pulled inside right before the door began to slide down.

Four armed men met the SUV and escorted the young women to the elevator where they rode up several floors.

A man wearing a navy blue suit was standing in the hall when the doors opened. "I'm Daniel. Nice to meet you. If you come this way, I'll bring you to the room."

After moving along a maze of hallways, the group stood before a metal door. Daniel knocked, stepped back, and gestured for Nell and Violet to enter. "I'll see you when you've finished."

Nell turned the knob and they went into the windowless room where a man stood next to a grouping of sofas. A wide smile crossed his face as he hurried over to shake the young women's hands. "Thank you for saving my life."

"It's nice to meet you, Adam. I mean, we met you before, but … it's nice to see you now that you're feeling better." A few tears gathered in Nell's eyes and she blushed at her flubbed greeting. "I'm Nell."

"I'm Violet." She shook with the man.

"You look great. Are you feeling well?" Nell asked.

"Amazingly well." Adam gestured to the sofas and they sat down together. "Please help yourself to drinks and cookies."

The three discussed the incident in the woods.

Nell said, "That's what we call it. The *incident in the woods*."

"I describe the experience using stronger words than that." Adam half-smiled and explained what had happened. "I panicked when Bonnie Plant showed me the pictures she'd taken of me at the beach. I nearly died when she told me she'd submitted the photo to an exhibition and it had won a prize. I knew it was over for me. I knew I had to run. I called the marshal assigned to me, but he didn't answer my calls or texts. A day later, I saw in the news he'd been murdered. That was it. I purchased things to disguise my appearance and I made a large withdrawal from my bank account. I needed cash because credit cards are too easy to trace. Honestly, I was sick to my stomach and scared to death for those few days. I knew the state park so I decided to hide out there for a while. I moved my stuff every day, tried to keep away from the popular trails."

Adam looked from Nell to Violet and his voice shook when he asked them, "Is Oscar okay?"

"Oscar's fine. We're taking care of him. We have another dog and they get along great. Oscar's a wonderful dog," Nell told him. "When we were in the woods and you were unconscious, Oscar stayed by your side the whole time. When the second gunman showed up, Oscar lay on top of you. He put his body over you to keep you safe."

Tears slipped from Adam's eyes and they tumbled down his cheeks. It took him a few moments before he could speak again. "I knew they'd come for me. I knew they'd kill Oscar. They're monsters. I decided to take him to Bluewater, to that great park there. We'd been to the park together a few times and the people with their dogs seemed nice. It killed me to leave him, but I knew someone would find him and make sure he'd be safe. I forgot to take his dog tags off his collar, but I couldn't go back to get them."

Nell and Violet told Adam how they found Oscar in the park. "We called the number on the tag. No one answered. We decided to take the dog to your house. We met your neighbors. When we went inside, things just didn't seem right."

Violet said, "We knew something was very wrong. When Oscar's things were found in the dumpster, we just knew you loved that dog and were doing something to try to protect him."

Adam brushed away his tears. "You were right. Oscar's been the one friend I could tell everything to, the one who understands me, the one who made me feel less lonely."

"You're being moved to someplace new?" Nell asked.

"I am. I don't like it, but if I want to stay alive, it's the only option I have." Adam took a deep breath and looked down at the floor. "I can't take Oscar with me. He's in that exhibition photo with me. If Oscar and I stay together, it would be easier for them to find us. People take their spouses and children into protection with them, but I can't risk it. If they find me, they'll kill my dog. I won't take that chance." He looked at Nell and Violet. "Will you promise me you'll find him a good home?"

"We already found one," Violet said.

"He's going to stay with us." Nell smiled. "We love that guy. If you ever want him back, tell your marshal. He's your dog first."

Adam's chin began to tremble. "Thank you."

Nell stood. "Before we say goodbye, there's someone else who wants to see you. Actually, two *someones*." She went to the door and opened it, and Oscar and Iris walked in looking a little apprehensive.

Adam got out of his seat, and when Oscar spotted him, he raced to the man and danced around him barking and jumping with joy. Adam knelt and hugged the dog and Oscar ran his tongue all over his face making Adam laugh.

Nell's and Violet's eyes welled up.

Mesmerized by the beauty of it, Nell watched the sparkling yellow and white particles pouring from Adam and Oscar swirl in long, wide ribbons around the room. Friendship, happiness, the pure, simple connection of love between two beings.

When the dog and the man had hugged and played and were sitting on the floor together, Nell introduced Iris to Adam, and then he and the two dogs played together for another fifteen minutes until a knock came on the door.

Adam's face fell. "It's time to go." He knelt beside Oscar and ran his hands over his dog's fur. "I have to go away, buddy. We can't be together. I don't want you to get hurt. I want you to be happy." He rested his cheek against the dog's head. "I love you, Oscar. Be a good boy. Live well with your new friends. I hope you understand."

Nell watched Oscar as he gazed up at Adam and she could feel and see the dog's emotions. "He does understand. He does."

The door opened, and Nell and Violet hugged Adam before the man wrapped Oscar in his arms one last time.

On the way out of the room, Oscar stopped and looked back for a moment, wagged his tail, and then followed Iris out into the hall.

Nell turned around. "Take care, Adam. Stay safe. We'll make sure Oscar is happy and loved."

The door closed, but the connection between the dog and the man would last forever.

Nell put her arm through her sister's as they followed the escort down the hallway to the elevator. "Come on, dogs. It's time to go home."

THANK YOU FOR READING!

Books by J.A. WHITING can be found here:
www.amazon.com/author/jawhiting

To hear about new books and book sales, please sign up for my mailing list at: www.jawhiting.com

Your email will never be sold, shared, or spammed.

If you enjoyed the book, please consider leaving a review. A few words are all that's needed. It would be very much appreciated.

BOOKS/SERIES BY J. A. WHITING

CLAIRE ROLLINS COZY MYSTERIES

LIN COFFIN COZY MYSTERIES

PAXTON PARK COZY MYSTERIES

SWEET COVE COZY MYSTERIES

OLIVIA MILLER MYSTERIES (not cozy)

SEEING COLORS MYSTERIES

ABOUT THE AUTHOR

J.A. Whiting lives with her family in Massachusetts. Whiting loves reading and writing mystery and suspense stories.

Visit / follow me at:
www.jawhiting.com
www.bookbub.com/authors/j-a-whiting
www.amazon.com/author/jawhiting
www.facebook.com/jawhitingauthor

Made in the USA
Middletown, DE
23 March 2020

86986732R00154